HOST OF EXTRAS

James Leasor

Chiselbury

Copyright © 2020 Estate of James Leasor

Published by
Chiselbury Publishing, a division of Woodstock Leasor Limited
www.chiselbury.com

This book is copyright material and must not be copied, reproduced, transferred, distributed, leased, licensed or publicly performed or used in any way except as specifically permitted by the publishers, as allowed under the terms and conditions under which it was purchased or as strictly permitted by applicable copyright law. Any unauthorised distribution or use of this text may be a direct infringement of the publisher's rights and those responsible may be liable in law accordingly.

First published 1973
This edition published 2020

For Jeremy

FOR SALE

TWO ROLLS, both believed unique, and collector's dream cars. First, Alpine, registered June 1915, fitted Grebel searchlights, leather shot-gun cases, pony-skin trunk, button upholstery; painted 14 coats Napier green with gold coach line; resilvered Zeiss spotlamps and Lucas 'King of the Road' headlamps, twin diver's helmet tail lamps. Whole car immaculate.

Second, 1914 London-Edinburgh tourer, grey coach-paint, red wheels and new red Connolly hide upholstery; new hood, tonneau and hood bag in best quality black duck specially piped in red. Ducellier headlamps with original glass reflectors, cut-out, fish-tail, altimeter, engine governor. Rarely used in wet weather.

Both cars in mint condition, stored in heated garage for years, impeccably maintained absolutely regardless of cost, and fitted host of extras too numerous to mention, unexpectedly offered owing to owner's sudden death. Serious enquiries only, no time wasters. Apply: Aristo Autos, Belgravia Mews, London, S.W.1.

PRELUDE

Jason Love, like most doctors, hated funerals. They were bad for his self esteem, for they reminded him of the inescapable truth, that death, the last enemy, must always win the last battle. And so whenever Love saw the long line of black, polished Daimlers, with discreet purple curtains on the bearer hearse, and the professional mutes in their swallow-tail coats and burnished top hats, he was reminded of the irony of Sir Thomas Browne's contention, that 'we all labour against our own cure, for death is the cure of all diseases'.

Usually, Love managed to avoid attending the funerals of his patients; the wreaths he invariably sent were deductible from tax, and time spent regarding the dead could be better employed helping the living. But, on this occasion, the dead man's son had particularly asked that he should attend, and since he had business in Minehead later that afternoon, he had been unable to find any convincing excuse.

So now he stood on the damp grass in the cemetery, feeling the chill of the cold earth seep through the soles of his shoes, while an adenoidal minister who had, so far as he knew, never even met this particular parishioner, intoned the words of the burial service, throwing a few grains of red Somerset earth on the lid of the polished coffin: 'Dust to dust . . . the Lord giveth and the Lord taketh away . . . blessed be the name of the Lord.'

Standing with his hands clasped in front of him, head bowed, Love allowed himself a sideways glance at the other mourners who had gathered on this bleak March afternoon to witness the burial of Nathaniel Rupert Doyle—'the laying to rest amid floral tributes', as the local paper was later to describe it.

Formerly an estate agent and now a dead weight, blood congealed in his veins, body wrapped incongruously in a white linen night shirt, hands folded piously across his chest, Doyle was beyond all earthly problems and concern.

As an estate agent, he had dealt mostly in small properties; rows of terrace houses to be sold at knock-down prices to property developers, usually men with dark skins, thick rings on their little fingers, and black tufts of hair on the backs of their hands. Men who used strong unplaceable accents, and with what Doyle would euphemistically refer to as 'North London connections'; which could mean anything from a share in an open-air second-hand car lot off the Edgware Road, to a more discreet interest in a protection racket among Mayfair gambling clubs.

He had lived in a large detached house between Minehead and Porlock; ran a Rover 2000; took three weeks' holiday in Raima every July and, latterly, a package trip with his wife for ten days in Klosters each January.

He had inherited the business from his father, and had done nothing, so far as Love knew, either to expand it or improve it. The tide of rising prices, with property values increasing tenfold in as many years, had carried him to prosperity on the crest of its waves. His office seemed the same as Love remembered it when he first visited him more than fifteen years earlier: dingy paint on the woodwork, a scuffed strip of carpet under his desk, brown lino in the corridors, and frosted glass panes to all partitions.

As the father of two sons, one an architect in Vancouver and the other, Henry, in the firm (and now standing staring down into the grave as though contemplating leaping, like Empedocles, into the hole), Doyle had been careful, cautious, timid and dull.

The parson ended his peroration, and wrung out his rheumatic blue hands. The wind lifted his surplice and threw rain in all their faces. The undertaker coughed noisily and bowed, and held out a hand to guide the widow back towards the waiting cars, where the drivers sat, heaters on, white beards of smoke growing at the exhaust pipes, anxious to be away to fill in their pools coupons. They had seen too many funerals for death to have any dignity.

Love's Cord roadster was parked a little way off. With its white paint, scarlet leather, twin amber-lensed Trippe spotlights, and *four huge outside exhaust pipes, it seemed so lively; so male, so vigorous, that it had no place among the cemetery cedars and yews and all the portents of the grave. He glanced surreptitiously at his watch; five to three. His appointment was for half-past; he would be in good -time.*

He shook hands with Mrs. Doyle before she was almost levered into the back of the undertaker's car, and then turned away. A hand touched his arm. Henry Doyle was behind him, his face unmarked by grief, or indeed, by any emotion whatever.

'Glad you could make it, doctor,' he said. 'Could I have a word?'

'Now?' asked Love. Should he not accompany his mother?

'If you have a moment.'

'Certainly. Where?'

'In my car, if you please.'

They crossed to 'the Rover that had belonged to his father. Love climbed in the front seat. Henry Doyle slid in behind the wheel and turned on the engine to boost the heater. It blew hot, dry, metallic breath over their knees.

'Thanks for everything you did for my father,' Doyle began.

'There wasn't, much I could do. In fact, nothing,' said Love, remembering the panic telephone call from Mrs. Doyle that her husband had fallen across the tea table and was breathing noisily.

'He had a great respect for you,' Doyle went on, running his left hand caressingly around the rim of the steering wheel. 'That's why I wondered if you could help me with some advice?'

'If I can.'

'I don't know how well you knew my father,' Doyle continued. 'But he had other interests besides his estate agency. At least, one other interest.'

'Really?'

This was not surprising. Love had listened to many unlikely tales of the unexpected aberrations and interests of middle-aged men; from the grocer who collected pink-edged knickers off local washing lines, to retired police sergeants and clergymen who spent whole days in Soho strip clubs. Pressure of an ageing prostate could produce all manner of sad and unimagined lusts. What could have been Nathaniel Doyle's other interest?

'He was very interested in old cars' Doyle went on.

'Old cars?'

Love could scarcely believe what he heard. The words touched an instant and entirely unexpected chord of affinity in his mind. Cars made in the twenties and thirties possessed a special attraction for so many people, for they possessed individuality and character that stood out in this later age of the second-rate and the mass-produced.

They had not been tacked together reluctantly and sullenly between unofficial strikes, but made by men who liked their work and had the craftsman's pride in 'the Daimler', 'the Vulcan', or 'the Bentley'. Cars then had been regarded as families' favoured servants, to be cherished for years; now they were like hired hands, to be got rid of at any whim.

'Old cars,' repeated Doyle. 'Can you imagine? And my mother knew nothing about it. She still doesn't. I only discovered it myself by chance, and knowing your interest in them yourself, doctor, 1 thought I'd have a word with you about it.'

The way he spoke made his father's interest sound like a disease.

'My father used to spend two or three days every month away from home. He told mother that he was inspecting properties or seeing one of the big landlords in London or Birmingham. We thought nothing of it. He'd done this for years.

'But then, through one of those coincidences that happen so often in life that you wonder if they're meant to happen, I was up in the Midlands seeing a landlord myself about some trouble with three shops he owns in Ilfracombe. I couldn't find his house at first, and I was driving through some suburbs, when, to my astonishment, I saw Dad's car parked in a side street. I thought it had been stolen. So I got out and waited by it, and then damn me if Dad didn't come out of a house.

'He was just as surprised to see me there as I was to see him. Only the previous evening, he'd said he was off to visit a landlord in

Chiswick. I was a bit suspicious, I can tell you. Thought he'd got a bird on the side.

'He could see the way my mind was working, so he let me into his secret. Took me round to a shed which he rented from the man in the house. And there were two damned great Rolls-Royces. Enormous things, with open bodies like huge baths, and buttons on the upholstery, and spidery wheels and lights all nickel-plated. . . . '

'Silver-plated,' corrected Love mechanically. One must be accurate. Of all possible hobbies to hold the secret attentions of the late Nathaniel Doyle, old cars seemed to be the most unlikely. But then, what had he expected, apart from some hidden vice? Years of dealing with human nature, in all its infinite cunning, had made him instinctively look for a dark answer to every question; a cheerful explanation invariably came as a surprise.

'Silver-plated, then, doctor', Doyle went on. 'And he'd owned these cars for years; since just after the war. Gave almost nothing for them: He used to drive up to the Midlands every month, and enter them in rallies under another name, wearing period costume. Bloody great coat like a Dickensian coachman. Cap with a button on top. Funny goggles. Gauntlets. The lot.

'Matter of fact, he got a great kick out of it. He'd a mass of newspaper cuttings about himself - as Mr. Stemaroyd - taking part in fetes for hospitals, driving film stars and T.V. celebrities to open new shops. Even acting as a chauffeur at a society wedding. Extraordinary.'

'Yes,' agreed Love, and remembering Nathaniel Doyle, it was. But it still did not add much to human knowledge, and he had an appointment to keep. 'Well, what can I do to help?'

'I want to get rid of those cars, doctor,' said Doyle. 'I don't know what they're worth, but presumably quite a lot. But if the tax people find out about them, then we'll be paying death duties on them.'

'Does your mother know about them?'

'No. They didn't get on too well, really, and I wouldn't like her to know that Dad has been so successful in keeping all this secret from her for probably twenty-five years. She'd only start to wonder what else he'd kept secret.'

'A good point,' agreed Love. 'So what can I do?'

'I could advertise them, of course,' said Doyle, paying no attention to him, almost thinking aloud. 'But I don't know what they're worth, and so I'd probably get done by someone who did. What I wanted to ask you, doctor, was, would you like to buy them?'

Love shook his head.

'You tempt me very much, Henry,' he said, 'but basically I'm a Cord aficionado. I admire the Rolls and the Bentley and the Delage and the Hispano and the Isotta and a lot more. But they don't do anything to me, not here in the heart, where it counts, when you're talking about old cars. I'm a Cord man. So thanks for the offer, but even if I could afford your father's cars, which I can't, I fear that these two Rolls-Royces would be wasted on me.'

'But not on someone else?' persisted Doyle anxiously.

'Of course not. I don't know what models they are. But they must be worth a lot to a collector or enthusiast. I could put you on to someone who'd handle them for you.'

'Is he honest?'

Love shrugged.

'How honest is honest? Do you put all your deals through the books? Or if someone gives you a five hundred deposit in cash because he hasn't a bank account, would you swear that this never goes into your back pocket, or your bureau drawer, and then appears in the accounts as a debt that was never paid? So not only do you get it tax free, but you have a tax loss as well?'

'Oh,' said Doyle, frowning, for that afternoon he planned to do just exactly this, but with five thousand pounds and not five hundred. 'That's getting a bit near the bone.'

'Exactly. The nearer the bone, the more tender the area of truth. My car dealer is honest in the broadest sense of the word. Put it like this. He might rape you. But at least he won't take the fillings from your teeth afterwards.'

'Is that a good recommendation?'

'In the old-car business, it's practically a written testimonial.'

'I'll have his name, then, doctor.'

Love took out a card.

'Here's his firm,' he said. He wrote down: Aristo Autos, Belgravia Mews, London, S.W.1.

'He's got a character there who helps him. Ex-tank sergeant called George. Talks in rhyming slang. I'd say he's also pretty honest. I met him first when I was a house surgeon at St. George's just after I'd qualified. Came in one day with a queasy appendix. We found out we both liked old cars. And I've kept in touch ever since. I buy any Cord spares they find, so we're in contact every month or so. Give my name to both of them.'

'Thanks,' said Doyle, opening the door for him. 'I will.'

CHAPTER ONE

I was sitting on my jack in my office, because there was no one else's jack I could sit on, when the telephone rang.

I let it ring for a while to make the caller think I might be tied up on another line, which is never bad for business.

The ambition of a property millionaire who I once parted from two thousand quid for a 1931 Daimler Double Six fitted with a commode, which I kidded him used to belong to a royal family - one of the old queens (the sort who wore a crown) - was to have *two* telephones in his Phantom V. Then, when friends rang, his secretary could ask them to hold as he was engaged on the other line. My ambition is simply to have my one line blocked with callers crazy to buy my old cars. One of the new cries of London: Cars to. sell, and who's to buy?

I should explain that, according to my letter-head, I am Aristo Autos. *'L'Etat c'est mot',* as Louis XIV said some years before me, and I deal in the more interesting makes and models of old cars. The mere fact that a car is old doesn't make it valuable, although many owners tell me otherwise. But if it is old *and* interesting, then maybe we can do a deal - at my valuation.

So I buy old cars at one price, tart them up and I sell them at another. If the second is greater than the first, I make a profit. If it's less, I make a loss. That's the story of business everywhere, but for my money (and no one else's is involved) the story of my life contains too many second prices not high enough to cover the first with comfort.

Many people, me among them, would not really call my office an office at all. It's not one of those modern affairs with acres of grey polished marble slabs, edged with anodised aluminium and black Swedish leather furniture on white nylon carpets. It's really a hutch the size of a privy or a telephone box, in one corner of a mews garage, about the only one left undeveloped in all Belgravia.

I rent the mews from some noble landlord, and it has room for four or five old cars, where horses used to stand on cobbles, and a bench and a pit. I've what I call a flat upstairs, but which others call less respectable names. But then lots of people call me names that aren't mine, so why get fussed about it?

I've nailed some enamel advertisements for Palmer Cord tyres and Pratt's High-Test petrol on the white-washed-brick walls, to add a touch of class - as the earl said when he put his hand on the barmaid's backside - and in my office I have a table with two drawers, which I keep padlocked, experience having taught me a low opinion of the intentions of my fellow men.

On this table stands the telephone, an ancient Oliver typewriter - the kind with keys that whack the carriage upside-down, like a parrot's beak-and a diary full of names and addresses of possible buyers and sellers of old cars. Right, then. *In res media* - into the middle of things, as Homer told his charioteer in the Athens rush-hour.

I picked up the telephone, and a voice said in my ear, having nowhere else to say anything: 'Are you Aristo Autos?'

Why do they always start like this?

'Of course,' I said. 'It's my pleasure.' At least, it isn't, but what's in a few words?

'I've been recommended to ring you by a Doctor Jason Love in Somerset. I believe you know him?'

'Very well,' I said. 'An old customer.'

In fact, he wasn't all that old, but he was a customer. Some men form attachments to cars instead of to women: sometimes as well as to women. They prefer a car of a certain type of colour, just as others hover round red-haired women or blondes.

Dr. Love has a thing about Cords, a car produced briefly and without great commercial success, between 1935 and 1937, by an astonishing American entrepreneur, Errett Lobban Cord. He had made a lot of money as a car salesman, dollying up Moon cars in fancy colours to flog them off when most other cars were black, and was after bigger deals.

The President of a bank that owned stock in the ailing car firm of Auburn, in Indiana, knew this and invited Cord to revive the patient. This he agreed to do, on condition that he had the option to buy stock at its low price if his policies succeeded. They did succeed, so he grew rich, bought out Duesenberg, then one of America's best made cars, and in 1929 marketed a front wheel drive car bearing his own name.

By the middle thirties, Cord was a millionaire controlling an aircraft company, fleets of taxis, and property by the mile, and decided to put out another model, under his own name. His hired hands whipped together a design with front wheel drive, concealed headlamps, vacuum gearchange, super-charged V-8 engine running back to front, the lot covered by a coffin-shaped bonnet with a metal Venetian blind stretched round the front. He might have made another fortune if early models hadn't been beset by unlucky snags like over-heating, and gears that jumped out on the over-run. Even so, the Cord was a lovesome thing to look at, if not quite so much fun to drive, as God and its owners knew very well.

I'd sold Love a Cord some years before, and any time I come across any bits or pieces for this curious mechanical abortion, I ring him at some out-of-the-way number in Somerset and he buys them. I reckon he must have a whole barn full of differentials and supercharger casings and all the other impedimenta that the true Cord lover collects. But then, like me, he's a bachelor, so he's no problem from a wife wanting to know *why* he needs more spares when he's already got about enough to build another car.

Therefore, I assured this character on the phone that I knew the good doctor well.

'He told me you were an honest man,' said the caller, almost accusingly, as though already suspecting a different state of affairs.

'I wouldn't disagree with that description. And how can I help you?'

Because there must be some way in which I could help him, or the nut wouldn't be breathing down the phone as though he'd been running a long way uphill.

'I have two cars to sell.'

And now it happens, I thought. Now he tells me. Two heaps of rusting rubbish held together by wormholes and moths' nests. I imagined the most uninspired vehicles I could think of: a Flying Standard Nine, and a Triumph Vanguard, or maybe even an old Singer, which few enough people wanted when they were new and, as with ugly women of slender means, no one wants when they grow old.

'What sort of cars?' I asked him carefully.

'Two Rolls-Royces,' he said. 'Open. I think they're Ghosts.'

This sounded so unlikely to me - two of them, remember - that I felt they could well belong to the spirit world. Then I took a deep breath and made the sign of the double cross, for this could be - just *might* be - my lucky day. I'd had so many unlucky ones that week that the tide must turn some time, or so the Good Book says; or some book.

'Where are they now, these monsters of yesteryear?'

I was still unconvinced this wasn't some kind of crank calling. But at least he hadn't reversed the charge, as too many of them try to do.

'I can take you to them,' said the caller. 'In the Midlands.'

'Take me,' I told him, as the old maid told the burglar. 'How much do you want for them?'

'Whatever they're worth,' he said, and paused. 'There's only one thing I should tell you. A small problem.'

'Ah,' I said. Why is it that in every old-car deal there always seems to be that small problem which sometimes grows so large it can throttle the whole thing? Some day, somewhere, in some happy land beyond the clouds, I must surely have a deal without any problems at all. Trouble is, we'll all be dead when we find it.

Dead lucky, as the croupier said of the gambler who had a heart attack through excitement when all his numbers came up.

'These cars belonged to my father. He's just died. No one knew he owned them, except me. I don't want them to appear in his estate, because they'll attract death duties.'

I like that word 'attract'. It's one that accountants and income tax inspectors use frequently. Which is another thing wrong with every deal: they attract tax as quickly as a magnet attracts jagged iron filings. But there are ways round it, and the Lord, in His infinite mercy, has been pleased to show some of these ways to me.

On the other hand, I didn't want to give away too much too soon, as. the choir girl told the verger, so I said, 'It's difficult to discuss this on the telephone, but the revenue people are very sympathetic.'

After all, this Adullamite might be a tax snooper for all I knew, although he had assured me he was an estate agent by the name of Henry Doyle.

He was actually, physically, in London, he said, and we could drive up to the Midlands (technically down, my old schoolmaster always told me you only went up to the capital city or to heaven). He would meet me at my convenience, he said.

'My convenience is the one in Theobalds Road,' I told him. 'Pick me up here instead. Then you can see the sort of cars I deal in.'

He said, 'Right,' and rang off. I squeezed a couple of blackheads at the side of my nose, watching myself in the mirror, wondering whether this was just a great big con. But if it were, what could this Henry Doyle hope to get out of it for himself?

I'm growing too old to make any more fruitless forays into the more depressing shires and suburbs to look for rubbish for sale at absurdly inflated prices. On the other hand, you have to move off your jack some time to get a deal, and this seemed as good a time as any.

I don't know whether I believed the caller but you can't argue against fact, and the fact is that, even today, after twenty years of combing the countryside for old cars to be renovated and sold at an inflated profit, they still keep on being discovered in the most unlikely places: in barns in mid-Wales, behind haystacks in Somerset, in Lincolnshire chicken coops. There are plenty of buyers but too little to sell them. After all, only a relatively few great cars were ever made, and most of them were cut about as tenders or ambulances during the war, so *if* this character really had two Rolls-Royces, we could both be very lucky.

I sat down and opened my mail while waiting for Doyle to arrive. I'd only received one letter that morning, apart from demands for rates, rent, water, telephone, electricity, gas, and a ludicrous communication from some ministry or other asking when I was going to send a man for industrial training. What man? I'd only George and, like me, he'd had his training years ago. The school of experience. A graduate from the great university of life.

The letter had come from a nut in Surrey, to whom I'd sold a Bean Tourer - not the most exciting car, even for Surrey, but then what did he expect for five hundred iron men? One of these Rolls I was going to see?

This flatheaded, web-footed friend ended his long complaint by saying that if he did not get satisfaction over this matter, he would put it into his solicitor's hands.

To which I typed a reply with two fingers in a Freudian way: 'Dear Sir, I have to hand (and foot) your letter regarding the sale of the Bean car. I note that you are dissatisfied with this transaction, and wish to put it in your solicitor's hands.

'So far as I am concerned, you can put *it* into your solicitor's hands or, indeed, into any other part of your solicitor's anatomy which your ingenuity can devise or which his compliance will permit. You have the honour to be, sir, my obedient servant.'

I felt better after that, and had a swig of Glen Grant, 10 Years Old whisky, of which I keep an emergency supply in one of the curiously shaped Essolube glass bottles they used to sell on garage forecourts thirty years ago (just as Dr. Love tells me he keeps an emergency reserve of his special brand in his surgery in a bottle marked 'Urine specimen. For pathological use only.').

I don't know how pathological his use was, but one thing I'll tell you; when I was younger, I used to drink to forget. Now, I drink to remember.

And what I remembered was a letter I'd received a few days earlier from my bank, begging to have my advice in re their letter of the 17th inst., regarding my overdraft.

Put in the simplest possible terms, I'd have to raise a couple of thousand quid faster than anyone was ever raised from the dead, or all manner of dire things would happen to me.

I unlocked the left-hand drawer, where I keep my traveller's cheques and loose tenners, counted out three hundred quids' worth of the latter, buttoned them in my back trouser pocket. Nothing like the rustle of notes to sway a reluctant seller; it beats the rustle of spring any day.

I picked up my briefcase, and checked that it contained a set of trade plates, a bundle of insurance forms to make out for any car I might drive, with a nest of spanners and some lengths of wire that come in useful in starting an engine that hasn't turned over since before your voice broke. Then, as George used to say when he was in the Army, I was ready in all respects to move off.

I hadn't much stock to sell, and what I had no one wanted to buy, so when Doyle did arrive, in a rented Cortina, I just gave him a quick glim over the two cars in the mews. The first was a Trojan. Not the horse, the car; a little square box with solid rear tyres on disc wheels the size of dustbin lids.

There was so much ingenuous ingenuity about the design that I thought it might interest him: a two-stroke engine living under the floor four feet away from its carburettor, which lurked beneath the bonnet; a hole cut under the rear seat so that, with a backward glance, the driver could see whether his rear light was lit, and so on.

My particular model was the Achilles, complete with warrior's head mascot on the radiator cap. The name was the car's only aristocratic feature, for the Trojan, on its solid rubber tyres, thin as tram lines, with a minute engine developing eleven horse power, and solid rear axle, was the epitome of inexpensive motoring in the nineteen twenties. As their advertisement asked: 'Can You Afford to Walk?'

Doyle appeared to think he could, for he walked over to the next, a 1933 Wolseley Daytona. This bore the name of the Florida beach where Henry Segrave and Malcolm Campbell had both won world land speed records, but the name was really the quickest thing about it.

For some reason, this very pretty little car had attracted the cads, the boulevardiers, and what all, in a big way. It was festooned with car club badges, aero screens, Mellotone horns, two bonnet straps, stone guards to the headlamp lenses, cooling louvres, two mascots, and even two spare wheels, as though the performance was so fierce that a keen driver might wear out both rear tyres in a great burst of speed.

Maybe the car's appearance, long, low, with two breast-like humps before the driver and the passenger, possessed a latent mammary attraction that unlocked doors in the minds of those who loved the kind of car (and girl?) that looked so much faster than it was.

These particular vehicles might not do much for me financially or psychologically, but at least they proved I dealt in old cars. Doyle glanced briefly at the framed photos of Isottas with tulip-wood bodies, French aerodynamic monstrosities of the thirties, with all four wheels enclosed, and Bentleys with instruments the size of soup plates, which I hoped proved the same thing; and then we set off, through the sad stretch of Failuresville ribbon development between London and the southern end of the M1.

Doyle was a thin, cold man, who bit his fingernails hard. Hair oil had stained his overcoat collar. He kept a paper bag of soft jelly-babies on the parcel shelf, and he slid out his left hand every few minutes for another green, yellow or red likeness of a child, chewing it noisily and licking his fingers.

I didn't take to him much, but there was no reason why I

should; he probably felt the same about me. Our relationship was to make money, not love, so I sat hunched up in my corner, puffing a Davidoff No 1, watching his face wrinkle in distaste as I filled the little car with smoke.

The day grew wetter the farther north we drove. I sometimes think it will rain forever in England, and then we will grow fins instead of feet and scales on our backsides, which could surprise some of our friends. We took the M45 exit into the wasteland south of Coventry. Soon this island will consist largely of concrete motorways leading to new council estates: rows of houses, all virtually the same design, stretching to a dreary, conforming infinity. I could only tell one from another by the colour of their curtains, and the fact that some windows framed a caged budgerigar while others exhibited a rubber plant in a pink plastic pot.

We stopped outside one of these nameless houses. The only thing that made it different from a thousand others was the fact that we had stopped outside it, and not the one next door.

'Where are the cars?' I asked him.

'Round the back. My father rented the shed.'

We walked back down three yards of garden path, through a wooden gate that grated on the paving stones, and up the road, to an alley between two houses. On one wall a notice advised readers: 'Commit no nuisance'. On the other, someone had chalked, 'Up the Spurs'. But why up them alone, and how far up?

The alley was rough with grey sodden cinders, and we picked our way through puddles pocked with rain. The gardens behind the houses were all that I had expected: twenty feet long, with sheds at the bottom, and rabbit hutches; others were littered with discarded prams or abandoned mattresses. This was tellyland. Any spare time you had, you spent watching a flickering window on a fictitious world that never was, is, or will be, before you ate your semi-defrosted fish fingers and your dehydrated vegetables, to which dye had been so expertly added.

At the third shed on the right, Doyle stopped, glanced around him as though he rather expected to be followed, and then opened the door.

'Shut it behind you,' he said. 'We don't want nosey parkers.'

Three shacks had been knocked together and the dividing walls removed, so the space under the eaves was considerable. It had to be, when you considered the cars, as we did, standing there, breathing in that strange old-car smell, that unique amalgam of coach varnish, oil that has dried on hot metal, real leather and cornauba wax polish.

At times like this, I don't want to sell cars. I just want to buy them to keep, and sometimes, in the evening and on my own, I'd sit in them, drawing infinite pleasure simply from the knowledge that I possessed the most perfect mechanical creation of its kind. So I stood there, my mouth hanging open like an offertory bag in a rich man's church.

'Well?' asked Doyle.

'They're good,' I told him, which was rather like admitting the Venus de Milo was quite pretty, only wasn't it a pity she'd such short arms.

These cars lacked nothing except me as their master. They were open Ghosts, just as he had said. The first was a light grey tourer with red upholstery. A London-Edinburgh, so-called because in 1911, Royce, after the death of Rolls, took up a challenge of his car's great rival, the Napier, to drive from London to Edinburgh in top gear only, and then to lap Brooklands and pass a fuel consumption test.

In that same year, with a single-seater body and a higher-geared back axle, a Rolls-Royce covered a quartermile stretch at Brooklands at 101 miles an hour.

The engine was quiet as an unwound watch - because it was under no stress at all, with tiny valves that let it take such delicate breaths of mixture, it never grew fussed like the engines of lesser breeds. It also had several silencers and, of course, a precision of build that has never been surpassed. As Royce prophesied, 'The quality will remain when the price is forgotten'.

The second car was an Alpine, with two searchlights, one on each side, huge boxes along the running boards, and leather gun cases in the rear compartment. Obviously, this had been built for some country gentleman or even a maharajah with a taste for shooting.

I call this an Alpine, like most other people in the business, although it was not the name that Rolls-Royce gave the car, but a reminder of the event that first made it famous, the 1913 Austrian Alpine trial, in which four Rolls-Royces entered, and covered the entire course of 1,645 miles without even needing a drop of water in their radiators. They would have finished in one, two, three, four order, if another car, not even in the trial, hadn't run into one of them, so they had to be content with first, second and third places.

Incidentally, many people think that the Ford Model T had the longest production run of any car-eighteen years. Rolls beat them on this, as on some other points, by being in production with the Silver Ghost for nineteen consecutive years. And in all that time no other car in the world has collected so many myths - all of which add to its value.

There's the story about the man who inherits a very old Rolls-Royce, and writes to the factory to see whether they'll recondition it. They reply saying they'd be most interested to do so, but since this is the only model they lack in their private collection, they'd be happy to give him a brand new Rolls in exchange.

Then there's the myth that all their engines are sealed, so that an owner can make no adjustments whatever, otherwise the company will object and somehow prevent it. They may object, but the only .time I remember them preventing anything was at the 1935 Paris Motor Show when a local coachbuilder put a very strange body on an open Rolls. This body had been copied from the 810 Cord - just like Dr. Love's - but married to the Parthenon-shaped radiator, it looked horrible. Rolls desired that it should be removed from the stand. It was.

These thoughts and some others chased themselves through my mind as I stood looking at the cars.

'What do you think, then?' asked Doyle nervously.

'I think they're very good,' I allowed.

'How much?'

I shrugged. This was always the question. How much is too much and how much is too little? If you know that, you know the secret of all commercial life. Long years of dealing with customers has made me cautious. I'll screw them if I can, but mostly they screw me like an electric drill if I give them half a chance.

'What do you want for them?' I countered.

'I don't know,' he said: 'That's why I asked Dr. Love if he could recommend someone who knew the market.'

I took a deep breath, which cost me nothing, and walked round the nearest car and kicked the tyre with the side of my shoe, while I thought what I should say next.

'If we put both these motors into an auction,' I told him, 'they'll fight against each other. Say a collector fancies one.'

'Right.'

'Then he sees the second, and at once he's not so sure he wants the first. They've got to go one at a time, or both together to one very rich buyer.

'I can't say what they're worth. It's a question of what they'll get. Since Dr. Love introduced you, my proposition is to let me take them back to my mews and check over them. The air's damp and corrosive up here - all these factory chimneys belching out chemicals - and then I'll sell them on commission.'

'How much commission?'

'Ten per cent flat, plus all my costs. And remember, these old cars are expensive toys. One of these beaded edge tyres can set you back fifty quid. This one I'm touching now looks pretty ropey.'

It did, too, with hairline cracks along the fish bone tread that had been fashionable fifty years, ago.

'Or twenty per cent if I bear all the costs, and take the risk they won't sell.'

'There's not much risk of that,'

'Maybe. *Eventually.* But not everyone can afford these things. You've got to wait your time. I may have to carry them round the country on a low loader to show them to someone who can't come to London. Or even cut in another dealer. It's not all cake, believe me. Anyhow, that's my offer.'

'You won't give me anything for them now, as they stand?'

'Sure,' I said, making a wild guess. 'I'll give you five thousand cash, the pair.'

I must know *someone* who could advance this on the promise of a fifty per cent split down the middle of the selling price?

Doyle said nothing, but stood biting his nails. I banged my hands together; it was cold in the shed. Also, I felt it was rather sad, being shut in that shabby clapboard hut with these magnificent mechanical monsters. They didn't belong to this dreary age, or to this subtopian hinterland of back-to-back houses and outside privies. They belonged to days of glory and nights of love: to the south of France before package-deal tourists ruined it; to palladian manors in Dorset, with two-mile-long gravel drives, raked every morning by undergardeners in green baize aprons; to liveried footmen and stillroom maids with white pinafores and starched caps pinned in their hair.

They were born into an age when the cars of the rich reflected the idiosyncrasies or individualities of their owners. The Maharajah of Indore, for instance, who bought the last Duesenberg chassis, had a Gurney Nutting roadster body built on it, with two sets of sidelights. One pair had red lenses; the other, blue.

He chose these colours so that, in India, his loyal subjects would know that if the car passed them with red lights on, then the Maharajah was driving; and, if blue, then the Maharani was at the wheel. And the second of only six or seven Bugatti Royales made - possibly the most expensive car ever conceived - was unusual because it had no lights whatever, either front or rear. This was because of the order of its owner, one Armand Esders, of Paris, who never drove at night. So what need had his car for lights? Now just try a car today equipped (or non-equipped) like this and see how far you go before the fuzz calls you to a halt.

These two Rolls were of that golden era, when the sun shone ever brightly on the British flag, when most of the atlas was coloured red - and the whole world was a much better place because of all these things.

To be arguing the toss over prices for such vehicles was unspeakable. As the original owners would have said, rightly shocked, if you have to consider the cost, you can't afford the cars.

'I'll think about it,' said Doyle, cautiously.

'Do that,' I said, glancing at my watch. We went outside. He locked the door and pulled the key to make sure it really was closed. We were halfway up the front path when he thought about it.

'I'll take your offer,' he said.

'Which one?'

'Twenty per cent commission. You pay everything out of that.'

We shook hands, an incongruous couple under the beady eye of the woman next door, who was peering round her net curtain at us, probably wondering what we'd been up to in the shed.

'You've got a deal,' I told Doyle. And he had.

More important, I'd got one myself.

CHAPTER TWO

When I told George how I'd arranged for two engineering students to drive these Rolls-Royces to London on tyres that had been old when he was young, and then we'd do them up before we sold them on commission, he looked as happy as a man who's been ducked under water three times and only surfaced twice.

'Unless some nutter takes them off our hands quickly, we'll be hearts of oak - broke,' he said, in his rhyming slang.

'Spring is in the air,' I assured him, also reassuring myself. 'London will be packed with Americans, all owning oil wells. You'll see.'

'Nose - I suppose.'

Then he went back to fitting a new set of leather bellows to an early SU carburettor I was trying to sell to a prove antique dealer as a study decoration.

Not a lot happened next day, either. According to an excited radio newsreader on my transistor, Peru had suffered a serious earthquake. Then, in Hong Kong the police were still seeking some crafty characters who had fused the lights at an international diamond exhibition and slipped away with a couple of million quid's worth of sparklers. Well, that was nothing to do with me either, although I rather wished it was.

At about five o'clock, the telephone rang. There was a pause, then a girl asked, 'Are you Aristo Autos? Hold the line please,' - all part of the crap that goes on when someone important, or someone who thinks he's important, which is not always the same thing, deigns to make a call.

A man's voice, wearing a mid-Atlantic accent, barked in my ear: 'This is Pagoda Films.'

He paused as though I should be impressed. It might have been impressive to him, so conceivably it could be to me. There was something religious about the name, like a temple.

I remembered an old line often used in novelettes, when young Berkeley Tremayne in his riding breeches had lured Deirdre La Fandanga down on the rocks and the surf was pounding away like his heart, and a vein throbbed in his temple. Come down to the temple and throb.

'What can I do for you?' I asked the caller, hoping it was nothing personal.

'Old cars,' he said briskly. 'I understand you deal in them. Could we hire half a dozen for a film?'

'For a price, yes.' I'd been bitten in this way before. Once, a film company had hired an old heap from me at a tenner a day, kept it for two months, and then only offered me one day's rent. When I protested, the producer pointed to the minuscule print on the back of the contract, where it said that ten pounds would only be paid for every day the car was what they called 'in shot'. Never again.

'Justin Amsterdam speaking. Pagoda. We're making a picture in Corsica. Adventure. Big thing. Host of extras.'

I recognised the phrase as one I'd often used in *Motor Sport* adverts when I had something to dispose of so laden with gadgets, like a Christmas tree: Mellotone horns, Klaxons, Marchals, Grebel signpost lamps, Brooklands silencers, 12" fishtails, altimeter *et al*. But whereas my extras were usually either chromium or nickel plated, Amsterdam's referred to human beings.

'The best of luck,' I said, feeling some enthusiasm was called for on my part.

'We need three cars,' he went on. 'Early nineteen-twenties, if possible. Open bodies. Sporty. You know?'

I knew.

'Of course,' I said mechanically, because if I didn't someone else would. 'Why not come round?'

'Will do,' he said, and replaced the phone.

He was standing in the mews within fifteen minutes. A shortish, fat man with thin hair, the colour of black Cherry Blossom boot polish, and a dark blue chin. He wore a camel-hair coat so thick it must have left many a brave camel bald. His shoes were polished like glass, and his soft, fleshy hands had never done any harder work than push a pen across a one-sided contract, or feel their careful way beneath a pretty girl's sweater.

As he moved, he left a faint dash of Brut on the air, soft as incense, but a whole lot more exclusive.

'Small place you've got here,' he said critically.

'That's right,' I told him, because it was. No mileage in arguing the point.

'Now, where are these cars?'

He came into my little office, holding his coat tight around his jacket in case it brushed the walls and dirtied it.

'I've got these for sale. Or I could rent them to you,' I told him, indicating the Trojan and the Wolseley.

'Too small,' he said. 'Not nearly impressive enough. We want cars as big as tanks. Damn great wheels. Lamps like searchlights. You know the sort of thing?'

'Perfectly.'

As we stood talking, I heard the flutter of old engines outside, faint as pheasant's feathers falling from a summer sky.

'They're here,' I said, congratulating myself on a nice piece of unexpected timing. 'I've had them brought specially for you from the Midlands.'

The engineering students were climbing down from their perches, stiff-legged after the ride, beating their arms about their bodies to restore the circulation. I had told them to drive with the hoods down. These old hoods have wooden sticks that grow brittle with age, and an amateur trying to raise them can do fifty pounds' worth of damage. But driving like that down the motorway makes you cold as the tip of an Eskimo's tool.

Amsterdam walked round the cars, looking at them critically.

'Are they reliable?' he asked at last.

'They will be before you hire them. But you've got to respect their age. They're not the sort of car you use to get the groceries in. Anyhow, have they got to run far?'

He shrugged his shoulders.

'Possibly. We may use them later for publicity round the country, as well as in the film.'

'These should be perfect, then,' I told him. 'Fifty years ago, they went over the Alps carrying five people and half a ton of luggage. They could do it again tomorrow. And the day after that. But not every day of the month.'

'Sounds like a husband's view of marriage,' he said. 'What rates do you charge?'

'Out of this country, a hundred quid a day. That covers insurance and any driver we supply. Plus living expenses, petrol, oil and repairs. Half to be paid in advance,' I went on. Always put your hard conditions at the beginning. It's too late to add any in afterwards. 'And all payments to be in dollar traveller's cheques.'

'Say I guaranteed you two weeks at a hundred a day?'

Keep on saying things like that, I thought. Aloud I said: 'Two thousand eight hundred quid in dollars. Put fourteen hundred on the deck and you've got a deal.'

He shook hands.

'Right,' he said. 'It's a pity you haven't a third - not even a Rolls, but just something exotic. However . . . We'd like you out there to be in charge. It's easier if anything goes wrong to have the owner on the spot. And you obviously know the temperaments of these old cars.'

I didn't tell him that I wasn't the owner, and I could already be in a difficult situation, if Doyle didn't agree to this idea.

'Let's have a letter confirming it, then,' I told Amsterdam.

'I'll send it round by hand.'

He couldn't well do it by foot, or mouth, even, I thought, wondering whether, like an old lover, he was all promises and no performance.

He shook hands, and stumped away up the cobbles.

I went back into my office and telephoned Doyle down in Somerset. It hurt to do it before six o'clock, when the cheap calls came in, but I had to reach him.

I wondered what his office was like, as I listened to the girl's thin, querulous voice at the other end, when she gave me the chat about Mr. Doyle being tied up, as though he were a fetishist, and what was I ringing in connection with, and all the usual rubbish telephonists say to try and fob off callers.

I reached Doyle finally and told him of Amsterdam's proposition, or at least as much of it as I felt he should know - literally half. After all, I was in this for a living, as the diver said when he jumped into the sea.

'We've had this offer,' I said. 'Guaranteed fifty quid a day for each car. Fourteen days. Makes a minimum of fourteen hundred quid, seven hundred to be paid down in dollars before a car moves out of this mews. What do you think?'

He thought so hard I could almost hear his brain revolve.

'Seems reasonable,' he allowed.

'It's more than reasonable. It's bloody marvellous, believe me. There'll be no record of the traveller's cheques - which means, Mr. Doyle, that you and your ever-loving wife, if you've got one, can go where you like round the world, regardless of any currency restrictions. And you won't have to pay any tax either, for it's cash. And there's another bonus to boot - or to shoe, if you prefer it.

'With a bit of luck, we can do at least as good a deal renting these cars again for publicity purposes when the film is made.'

'I'll be guided by what you say,' said Doyle, which told me he'd nothing to say himself.

'I say we do it, then.'

At this rate, I couldn't lose. Nice work, if you can get it. And I was getting it. The money, I mean.

'Drop me a note,' I told him. 'I'd like to have your O.K. in writing. Meanwhile, I'll insure the cars, so you can't lose. Then if they both burn to the ground, we're still quids in.'

And we were. There was only one tiny snag. Pagoda's credit rating. I owed my bank so much money I didn't like to ring them up and ask them to check on someone else, and, in any case, what use is a bank check? They would simply reply very cautiously that 'P.F. . . . Ltd is a respectable account, introduced to us by a valued customer. We have no reason to believe they would enter into commitments they could not fulfil.'

Less charitable people can think of all sorts of reasons why people enter into commitments they have neither hope, intention nor even imagination of fulfilling, but bank clerks don't think like that. If they had that sort of imagination, they'd be making their own money, not dealing in other people's.

I decided to do my own check, locked up the garage and walked across the mews, because there was no other way of crossing it, save on hands and knees, and gave a shout outside Jacko Jackson's home.

At least, he called it home. To me, it seemed more like a night refuge from the elements. Two rooms, once used by a groom, with whitewashed boards around the walls, above another garage where one of the more successful Harley Street abortionists kept his Corniche.

Jacko Jackson, like many of us, had chosen a hard way to make an easy living. He called himself an actor, although on the charge sheets of innumerable provincial police courts, after he had been apprehended in local public parks or lavatories, wearing a raincoat and with his flies undone, he was more accurately described as 'of independent means'. In fact, he dodged about on the fringes of show business and the used-car trade like an ageing blue-arsed fly.

I'd heard he'd been well educated years ago, and he had a certain roguish impressiveness about his face, which, like Milton's Beelzebub, was majestic though in ruin. As such he was in some demand, though riot as much as he'd like to be, taking the part of ambassadors or admirals or white-haired butlers in TV ads for dog foods and unlikely British wines that had never known a grape. This was Jacko's show business side.

So far as car dealing was concerned, when one of us took in a Rolls that was just too new to sell as vintage, and yet too decrepit to renovate entirely, we would re-register it in the fictitious name of some ecclesiastical dignitary, such as the Bishop of Balls Pond Road, or the Rural Dean of Nately Scures.

Then Jacko, using a chauffeur's uniform he'd kept after one of the commercials when he'd been the driver of a wedding car, would trundle this ancient heap of woodworm and rotting metal to prospective buyers in the shires, who'd read our come-on advert in *The Times,* about a one-owner car, schedule serviced, always chauffeur driven, late property of a bishop.

He'd have a quick gander beforehand in *Who's Who* or *Burke's* to check on the fellow's old school tie, so he could say that his former lordship, the bishop, had expressed a dying wish that the car should go to another Old Etonian.

Sometimes, when he was sober enough, Jacko would appear as the owner himself, wearing an Old Harrovian or Marlburian tie and a bit of pancake make-up to dim the shine on the end of his nose. Then he'd be selling the car to pay his son's school fees, or to set his daughter up in business because a cad had let her down.

I had also often used him in other ways. Say I am having difficulty persuading some flathead to buy an ancient chariot for £3,000. I engage Jacko to arrive in a (hired) Rolls, wearing a (hired) camel hair coat and soft brown hat and silk tie he has picked up somewhere.

In an accent rich and sweet as dark brown fruit cake, he informs both of us that thirty years ago he owned this actual car and for sentimental reasons he will pay me a thousand more than I am asking – immediately - if only I will sell it to him.

I explain, very embarrassed, that much as I would like to accept this astonishing offer, I am morally bound to this character who's having difficulty in making up his mind. This flathead now immediately loses all his hesitation. If this car is worth £4,000 to someone else, it *must* be worth £3,000 to him. Why, he could make a thousand on the deal. So avarice overcomes inertia. He buys immediately. Jacko gives him his card, and begs him to get in touch, should he ever wish to sell.

Of course, the man gets in touch, probably that same day, but the card is only an accommodation address, and one more sucker has learned that life can be hard and rough.

Jacko boasted that he kept his ear so close to the ground in the motor trade and all the peripheries thereof, that he practically lived lying on his right-hand side. And some of his worst moments in court stemmed from explaining why a prowling constable had caught him in exactly that position.

As I beat on the door now, his watery old face, soaked by a generation of cheap gin, peered woozily out of the window above me, like a blown-up version of those little wooden weathermen that go in and out of a house when it's going to rain.

'I'm not selling anything,' I told him. 'I'm giving it away.'

'Oh, it's you,' he said, relieved. 'You'd better come on up. But I warn you, I've got nothing to drink.'

He'd drunk it all himself, of course. I knew that. He was waiting for me at the top of the steep, unpainted stairs, half drunk, shuffling in carpet slippers, the left with a hole cut in it to accommodate a bunion. As an ambassador or admiral off-duty, Jacko looked unconvincing.

'What news?' he asked, licking his lips.

I could smell gin on his breath at seventeen feet. Close-up, he could have distilled new spirit simply by breathing into a glass of water.

'Fellow called Amsterdam. Claims to be in films. Pagoda Films. Ever heard of either of them?'

'They don't make TV commercials, do they?'

'I don't know what they make,' I told him. 'All I want is to make some money out of them. They are hiring two old Rolls I've just picked up. In Corsica. Are they sound?'

He looked at me more closely then, eyes focusing on me reluctantly, irises trembling like holes in a moth's wings.

A horrible thought struck both of us at the same time. This could easily be an elaborate scheme for picking up two expensive old cars and then selling them abroad. There are so many rogues around that you can only tell honest men because they have hair in the palms of their hands.

'I'll make enquiries,' he said. 'What's it worth?'

'A tenner,' I told him. 'Tonight.'

'Tomorrow,' he said. 'I'm away flogging an old Facel Vega tonight. Late property of famous actor. I'm his uncle tonight.'

'Then I hope you're my informant tomorrow.'

And at ten on the following morning, Jacko's vinous voice, hoarse as Bacchus with a hangover, was breathing through the telephone into my ear.

'That Pagoda bit,' he said. 'New company. One pound job. Justin Amsterdam owns two shares. Another man, Robert Black, described as of independent means, owns one. Registered address is a lawyer's office in Golders Green. Nothing more known.'

'Have they ever made a film?'

'No. But there's always a first time. And this could be that.'

'Could be,' I agreed. 'Anyway, drop on over. I've ten iron men here itching to buy you a drink.'

I put back the receiver, lit a cheroot and lay looking up at the ceiling, wheels in my mind beginning to mesh. .

Years ago, a film company would have meant Rank or MGM, or Twentieth Century. Now it meant two or three sharp characters with long hair, an idea and maybe an option on a star or a director. Pagoda was probably no better and no worse. The only thing I liked about them was that they were offering me money, but I wanted to make certain they had money to offer.

I swung myself out of bed, shuffled into the kitchen, threw two raw eggs in a bowl and beat them to a pulp with some Worcester sauce and orange juice. I read somewhere that this contains all the vitamins necessary for a full day's work. I don't know whether the fellow who claimed this knew what he was talking about, or what his day's work consisted of, but it tastes so foul you feel it must be doing you good. Nothing so vile could conceivably do you any harm.

Then I went downstairs, picked up the letters, and unlocked the door for George. He was late that morning, picking up some spares from a breaker's yard in Willesden.

The only envelope of interest had an embossed address, Pagoda Films Ltd. in Curzon Street, with so much raised gold on the paper I thought they must be robbing their teeth.

Presumably they'd still left some gold in the bank, for it contained a letter signed by Amsterdam agreeing to the terms we'd discussed. It was all simple and straightforward, none of the usual arguing about conditions. The main thing was that Amsterdam wanted the cars to be ready by the following Monday, five days ahead. No problem there. Altogether this looked an honest proposal, which made, a change, a welcome flash in the pan, as the man said when he threw a firework into his neighbour's crapper.

On the afternoon of the third day after the Rolls arrived - a touch of the old Genesis there - Jacko Jackson dragged his jack across the mews and into my office. I opened the right-hand drawer, and took out a flat medicine bottle of gin I kept ready filled for him.

He put it in his pocket without a word.

'Bit more news,' he said. 'Pagoda Films. I hear on the jungle drums, Amsterdam's credit is good. He's got real money behind him.'

'Whose real money?'

Where there is a thickness of the folding stuff, I like to know who provides it, because maybe they could then also provide some for me. Once I made seven hundred quid cash out of an interior decorator who wanted a client's study done out with four old radiators from a Rolls, a Bentley, a Hispano, and a Delage - all linked together with pipes to make a central heating system. He could have bought them all for two hundred, if he'd known where to go for them. You never know your luck - so long as you know your market.

'I'm not sure,' said Jacko, 'but they've definitely got it there, boyo.' He was going to say more, when he paused, bottle halfway to his mouth.

We both heard footsteps at the same time.

'You've got company,' he said, 'or a customer. I'll scarper.'

Jacko scarpered very slowly, like a stiff-legged black beetle with alcohol in his veins.

A girl stood waiting outside on the cobbles. She might have been twenty or twenty-five, or again, she might have been beneath the age of consent. You never can be sure now when the young want to look old and the old look terribly, terribly young. She looked terribly, terribly screwable to me.

'I am Victoria Bassett,' she announced. 'I've come from Mr. Amsterdam. I'm going to drive one of these old cars.'

'Which one?' I asked her.

'The green one,' she said immediately, looking at the Alpine. 'It matches my eyes.'

I looked at her eyes. She was right. They were green as the sea when the sun goes in over the top of the hill. I wouldn't mind going in over the top of the hill with her. I wouldn't say she was green, either.

'They're heavy to hold on a corner, you know,' I warned her. 'Have you ever driven one?'

'Yes. Years ago. My grandfather used to have a Ghost.'

I didn't argue with that. He was probably a ghost himself by now.

'We'll try it up the road, first,' I said, meaning the car, and not anything else. She climbed in behind the wheel, glanced over the dash, set the ignition lever on the steering column to 'late' - only in lesser breeds of old car is this timing device labelled 'advance' or 'retard'. Then she switched on the magneto, climbed out of the car, walked round the silver Parthenon-shaped radiator, and gave the crank handle a sharp upward swing.

The engine sighed into life, quietly as the breathing of a sleeping child. Victoria climbed back behind the wheel, watched the oil gauge needle trembling against its dial, then leaned down, and pulled out the heavy screwdriver George had wedged between the clutch pedal and the bearing housing, to keep the conical facings of the clutch from gumming together when the car was standing. She put her foot on the clutch, flicked the outside gear lever into first, and looked at me. She knew a bit about old cars, all right. I wondered who had taught her.

I climbed up beside her and we puttered out of the mews into the thick thrombosis of traffic. There was no space for speed, and I noted approvingly that she pushed the governor lever to the end of its quadrant - an ingenious device to hold the car at a set speed, uphill, downhill, regardless of the load, the weather, the traffic, and, like so many other old inventions, now hailed as new.

'How far must I drive to prove I can cope?' she asked me, after a few minutes.

'You can,' I told her. We turned back towards my mews.

'You'll have a coffee?' I asked her, as we stopped outside the garage.

'If you're having one.'

She followed me up the stairs. I threw two spoons of Nescafe and sugar into a pan, and boiled up some milk. We stood drinking it out of tooth mugs, watching each other. Her eyes flitted around the room, hanging price-tags on everything. I couldn't quite place her, either.

'Do a lot of film work?' I asked her.

'No. Not a lot.'

'What is your usual line of country, then?'

'Oh, odd things. A bit of modelling sometimes. Help a friend who runs a riding school. I've even been a package tour courier. Someone told me Justin Amsterdam needed a driver-and also a double for some long shots of a girl in an old car. So I rang him. Amsterdam had a look at me - and here I am.'

'Right. Well, leave me your phone number. We're to be ready to go by Monday, but I may want to contact you before then.'

We finished our coffee, she wrote down her number on my

memo pad, and left.

I went downstairs after her to my task of making money in the hardest possible way: by working for it.

CHAPTER THREE

Amsterdam's letter did not arrive next day - only bills come in promptly – but it came the day after, with a banker's order for fourteen hundred dollars on the London office of the Chase Manhattan. I was to collect the remainder from his flat in Cumberland Terrace, in traveller's cheques, as agreed, at three o'clock that afternoon.

I couldn't make it at three. I had to see a customer who had been deluded enough to buy a Singer Junior from me and now wanted his money back because he said the car wouldn't do more than forty-five miles an hour downhill. I'd spent his money, so I had to convince him that he must have been driving against the wind. I told him he was fortunate he had not bought a Peugeot Bebe, which was one of Bugatti's earliest designs. Its power was so low that if the driver ran head on into a strong breeze, his car stopped entirely. He went away, not entirely convinced.

It was thus nearly five by the time I was tarting myself up, brushing my hair in the driving mirror of an Essex Super-Six, when I heard a trumpet blast in the mews outside that could only come from a pair of three-foot Stentor horns. I knew only one car fitted with these. A Cord. And only one man in England owned the open white 812 roadster that stood outside my garage. Dr. Jason Love.

He wore a flying jacket and tweed cap and was peeling off a pair of calfskin driving gloves; a tallish man in his late thirties, with blue eyes. He threw the gloves into the car.

'You're a long way from your patients, doctor,' I told him as we shook hands.

He nodded.

'And I'm increasing the distance smartly. I have to see a specialist in Wimpole Street with one of them tomorrow morning.

Then I'm off to the South of France for two weeks. As I was in town, I thought I'd call to ask whether Doyle had contacted you.'

'Come inside,' I told him.

He walked into the garage and looked admiringly at the old cars.

'I see he has.'

'Yes,' I said. 'I've had another bit of luck, too. I'm hiring them out to a film company. Two weeks guaranteed, on location. Corsica. All expenses paid.'

'Which should be better than a belt up the jack with a hobnailed boot,' said Love approvingly, kicking a tyre absent-mindedly.

I agreed, it was even better than a belt from a hand-sewn shoe.

'Anyway,' Love went on. 'This is a professional visit as much as a social call. I've an exhaust blow on the left bank.'

He didn't mean the one in Paris, but the left-hand set of cylinders in his V-8 engine.

'Could you cut a new gasket?'

'I couldn't, but George can,' I told him, and whistled George up from the pit, like some bald-headed Mephistopheles.

'I'll be at my club overnight,' said Love. 'If someone could run the car round there, say at about half-past eight, tomorrow?'

'Will do,' I promised; 'And have the repair on me. I owe you that at least for your introduction to Doyle.'

'Thanks,' said Love, obviously pleased. He had not expected this. Gratitude is sufficiently rare to cause surprise in those who find it, which is my thought for today, and every other day, too. It also happens to be true.

I watched Love walk up the mews, then drank five fingers of Glen Grant from the Essolube bottle, and folded myself into my SS 100, and headed out against the evening traffic towards Regent's Park.

I'd like to be rich and live in Cumberland Terrace. To wake up in the morning, and look out from wide windows in high-ceilinged rooms across acres of grass that might be part of your country estate, but is actually a whole lot better because you haven't got to pay for its upkeep.

You can walk two hundred yards down the road and be in an Underground train if you don't catch a cab. *Rus in urbes,* as my Latin master used to say, when he wasn't prophesying doom and the dole for me. The best of both worlds, as the old lecher put it, when he squeezed the beauty queen's 42-inch knockers in his trembling hands.

I pulled into the Terrace behind a blue Rolls with armorial bearings on the rear doors, and a red E-Type with the chauffeur doing his pools at the wheel.

Some of the houses had been split up into flats, with several names above bell-pushes. Amsterdam's was one of these. As I pressed the bell beneath his name, the door opened. A man came out, wearing an unbuttoned raincoat with a scarlet silk lining. He might have been a boxer years before, or a professional footballer who had become a successful betting shop owner. He was still good-looking, but just on the wane, running to fat. He climbed into the E-Type, and the chauffeur went off as though he had a couple of laps to make up at Le Mans.

I walked up to the second floor. The front door of Amsterdam's flat was open, but I knocked on it and called 'Shop!' just in case he might not be expecting anyone. When you're taking money off someone you don't want to barge in on him unannounced, just in case he's amusing himself in some private way, like introducing Fagin to a young girl grateful for the introduction.

I thought I heard a vague reply from a distant, inner room, and went in, over a sea of green Wilton, with white Aubussons piled as thickly as if we were in Heal's carpet section. The easy chairs and settees were, predictably, all black-buttoned leather. One wall was a mass of books bound in red and green and dark blue leather, with the names in gold.

I called again. This time, someone answered, but not in any intelligible tongue.

I waded through the carpet into the next room. A study, with a desk big as a billiard table supporting shaded green reading lights, swivel chairs, two tape recorders and three telephones: all the stock impedimenta of the rich tycoon, or the man who would like to be thought both.

I saw all this, but only as background, for lying in the chair behind the desk, head back, blood and vomit down his chin and over the lapels of his Squires' hundred-guinea suit and his Harvie and Hudson striped silk shirt, lay Mr. Amsterdam.

He was not dead, only half-conscious, one hand scrabbling as though his five fingers had a mind of their own, trying to reach the nearest telephone, and never quite making it.

Near the desk was a French gold and glass circular table packed with drinks. I poured out some whisky, added soda .and held the glass to his lips. Dr. Love might not have approved, but then he wasn't there. Amsterdam didn't think so badly of the gesture. He struggled upright, coughed out some gobbets of blood, wiped his mouth with a silk handkerchief, and drank greedily.

'What happened?' I asked.

'I was attacked,' he explained, nodding towards the empty glass.

I refilled it.

'Bloody stunt man. We had an argument. You probably saw him on the way up?'

Amsterdam paused, as though he was going to say more, then decided against it. I remembered the big man running out of the front door. I'd remember him again.

'I'll have a wash and change,' he went on. 'I've some money for you. Stay around.'

He went out of the room, and then I heard a shower running somewhere. He was back in five minutes - hair sleeked down, a touch of talcum around his black eye - wearing a white silk polo-neck sweater, dark trousers and sandals. He poured himself another drink, and this time offered me one.

'What happened?' I asked him.

'He wanted to come to Corsica. I simply couldn't use him and told him so. He got a bit agitated. However, I'm insured. I tell my ex-wives I'm worth more dead than alive. But not, you understand, necessarily to them. You married?'

I shook my head.

'My hat's on my head, my troubles are covered.'

'A very prudent philosophy. Now, this money. Fourteen hundred quid in dollars, wasn't it?'

'It still is.' He knew this as well as I did.

Amsterdam took a key ring on a gold mesh lead from his pocket, unlocked his desk, removed an envelope, shook out a thousand dollars' worth of traveller's cheques, and some odd fifty-dollar bills and smaller change-and pushed them all towards me. I counted them, then scooped them up into my back pocket.

'Here's the plan,' he went on, opening a folder on his desk.

'I want those cars at Marseilles by the twentieth to catch the ferry to Ajaccio. I've chartered a plane for them at Luton. I'll give you all the details tomorrow. Pity you've only two old cars, though. As I said at the beginning, I wanted several. You couldn't rustle up some more?'

He pushed a box of Davidoffs towards me, took one himself, lit it, felt his nose tenderly: it must have been hurting him more than he cared to admit.

'You're not giving me much time,' I pointed out.

'That's another thing I need. Time,' he said wearily.

'You also need a doctor,' I told him. 'And I know the man.'

'I have my own. I'll see him tomorrow.'

'*My* doctor starts two weeks' holiday tomorrow night. He's also an old-car fanatic. Runs a Cord. Why not take him - and his car? The only supercharged roadster left in the country.'

'Would he come?'

Amsterdam looked at me quizzically, turning the idea over in his mind. For some reason, it seemed to appeal to him.

'I could ask him,' I said. 'Say, free holiday, living expenses, plus fifty quid a day walkabout money. He just might be interested in it. I'll ring him now.'

He nodded towards the third phone, I picked it up, dialled Love's club. He was paged, and I explained the proposition to him, and doubled the fifty walk-about money to a hundred as I did so. Think big, as the guy with the fifteen-inch weapon told the fellow with the pee-shooter. Love liked the idea.

So we fixed it up.

I skated back to Belgravia Mews in my SS 100, humming to myself like a happy top.

It was one of those evenings when even the sun seems reluctant to go to bed, because he has to sleep alone; when all the girls in London are wearing summery see-through dresses, and young men with string-backed gloves, eyeballs hanging out, coagulate in the King's Road, cruising up and down in their open MGBs and Lotus Elans, watching all the tail go by.

I had to see a man about an Amilcar down in South London, and when I reached his house, his wife said I wasn't expected until tomorrow, and her husband was out and she didn't know where he was. So I hung around for an hour and then, when he still didn't return, I drove back home. Another wasted evening.

My mews is so small that a couple of cars standing in it can make a crowd. A little way up from me was a red E-Type with a chauffeur reading the evening paper at the wheel. I remembered the number; you have to, in my business. Sometimes you are offered two different cars that inexplicably carry the same number, which makes you wary.

It was the Jaguar I had seen parked outside Amsterdam's flat; the chauffeur had been doing his pools then. Better than doing his nut, of course, but if I'd been hiring him, he would have been polishing the car or working a knitting machine, or otherwise doing something useful in his employer's time.

He didn't notice me, and I didn't eye him; I'm not that way inclined. I let myself in through the wicket gate, drove the SS into the garage and slammed the door shut. The two Rolls stood bonnet to tail, almost filling the space behind my other cars. I don't know why I walked over to them; maybe it was the fact that one of the front left-hand bonnet fasteners on the Alpine was open, and I do not like untidiness of that sort. Neither did George.

I opened the bonnet and looked at the engine. It had been wiped clean and all the copper pipes and aluminium castings and silver-plated nuts were polished. But somehow the polish has been hasty; there were small smears of oil down one side of the block, and I couldn't think why. The engine was spotless by any standards, save George's standards. Maybe he was ill? Then I remembered: he was due to go to Portsmouth for two days to see his only relation, an aged aunt. Perhaps the thought of this had made him skimp his work?

I lowered the bonnet, tightened both fasteners and walked thoughtfully up the stairs.

I saw the man in my room before he saw me. This wasn't surprising, because he was sitting in the only easy chair, smoking one of my cheroots, and had his back to me. He didn't get up when I entered the room, which showed, he had bad manners, but he turned and looked at me. He was the man I had seen in Cumberland Terrace, the stunt man who had beaten up Amsterdam. Close to, his face was thick and bloated, as though someone had taken a bicycle pump to a stock handsome face and increased the nose and lips and cheeks and ears just that little bit larger than life. He had an impressive spread across the shoulders. His raincoat was still open and his suit was cut to hide an equally impressive spread across his gut. For a stunt man this could mean problems.

'I hope you don't mind,' he said, with the air of one who didn't give a fish's tit if I did. 'I didn't want to wait in the car, so I came up.'

'My door was locked,' I told him.

He smiled and pulled out a key with a lot of little nicks in it.

'This opens anything,' he boasted.

'Not my legs, it doesn't,' I told him. 'And who are you?'

I might as well know who I was going to throw down the stairs.

'I saw you going into Amsterdam's flat,' he went on, not answering my question. 'I checked up the number of your car. That gave me this address. I'd like to make you a proposition.'

'Make it,' I said, 'and if I don't like it, beat it.'

'Five hundred pounds,' he said, putting his left hand into his inside jacket pocket, 'payable half now, half through the post tomorrow morning.'

'For doing what?' I asked him.

'I'll be frank,' said the man, which meant he was going to lie; Frank doesn't live here any more.

'There's a stunt job going in Amsterdam's new film. I'm getting too old for some of the harder work - high diving, jumping off trains and so on - but this particular trick's fairly straight. And there's a bit of acting to it as well. You don't need talent to act in films - only the physique and the ability to photograph well. I've got both. But I need this chance to prove it.'

'So why did you give Amsterdam a black eye?'

'Because he wants to hire someone else.'

'It's up to him, if he's paying the money.'

'He's not signed anyone definitely yet. If I'm there, I'll get the part. He's too mean to pay two of us.'

'Why are you offering me five hundred pounds?'

'To stand down from driving your old car. To let me take your place. Amsterdam won't know until he arrives and sees me there.'

'No go,' I said.

'Five hundred's a lot of money,' he said.

'Those cars are worth a lot more. Also, they're not mine. I have to be there to see they're well treated.'

'What if you couldn't go? What if you were ill? If you had an accident?'

'That would be different,' I agreed.

'I mightn't have to pay you five hundred then,' he said musingly, and came up with his elastic-sided boot, right in my crotch.

At least he would have done, if I'd kept my vitals where they were, but I saw his eyes narrow almost imperceptibly as the message to attack telegraphed from his boozy brain, and I jumped back.

As his foot came up I seized his shoe and twisted it first to the right and then sharply to the left. His head butted me in the gut. I brought down my right hand across the back of his neck, but I might as well have been hitting meat on a butcher's counter. He had flab, but his skull was solid, like his brain.

However, one does not travel through life's journey as an old-car dealer without learning some of the basic rules of self-defence; not infrequently clients show dissatisfaction violently. I brought my left knee up to his nose, and we both struggled back, sobbing for breath. I couldn't understand the crudeness of his approach. If someone won't do something for a set sum then you should increase your offer, not literally attempt to beat him down.

'You stupid bastard,' he panted.

'I don't think I want you as an employer,' I told him.

Suddenly he heaved back his shoulders and threw off his coat, meaning to come in for the hard stuff. In that moment, as both his arms were stuck in his sleeves, I hit him, not on the nose or the jaw, but on the Adam's apple. He gave a great bubbling sob of pain. His face turned blue and he sagged, going down on his hands and knees, still struggling, his arms in his sleeves.

Then one wall of the flat came away and hit me on the side of the head.

Through a red haze of pain, and from a position of prayer on my knees beside him, I saw the chauffeur. He had come upstairs behind me and I had not heard his rubber-soled shoes.

He was pulling back his right shoe now to put it into my temple for the second time. And there was nothing I could do to stop him, nothing at all.

I couldn't even speak. I just crouched, watching, like Fido the dog, and as I watched, like someone in a dream, I saw the chauffeur's face fold in on itself and his eyes roll up. His foot lost all impetus and he dropped, like a sack of clothes, on the floor beside me. I moved over a few inches to give him space. I don't like to be hemmed in.

A third man had come into the room. Dr. Love.

'You have problems?' he asked me.

I nodded.

'Uninvited guests,' I said.

He helped me to my feet.

'Do you want to press charges?'

'I'd rather press their balls in a vice."

'That comes later,' he said. 'Business before pleasure.'

He was always the urbane one, this Love.

'You seem in one piece, anyhow, and still agreeably pugnacious. Have a drink. I prescribe some of your own whisky. For medicinal purposes only, of course.'

He poured out two glasses. We both drank. The two men on the floor began to crawl away. I trod on the stunt man's fingers with my shoe and turned the steel-edged heel into the knuckles. He stopped crawling, and his face creased in silent agony, to show how he'd look in thirty years' time, wrinkled as a serpent's scrotum.

Love sat down in the chair and lit a Gitane.

'What I like about London,' he said conversationally, 'is that here it's all *happening.* Things are so quiet in the country that if you hear a noise, you don't know whether it's a man or beast.'

'Here you can bet it's a beast,' I said grimly. 'Two beasts who walk like men are with us in this room.'

The chauffeur stirred as though from deep slumber.

'Who are they?' asked Love.

'The creature I've just trodden on says he's a film stunt man. He offered me five hundred iron men to drive one of the cars instead of me. When I refused his offer, he set about me to try and make me change my mind. The other man is supposed to be his chauffeur.'

'Do you know them?'

I was going to shake my head, but it felt so sore, that I didn't even bother.

'No,' I said. Then I remembered Jacko Jackson, who lives over the road; he knows everyone, including many who say they have never met him.

'We should have them identified,' said Love, as though he was speaking of two pathological specimens that had unexpectedly turned up in a patient's water.

I picked up the telephone and dialled Jackson's number. His voice answered through a mellow haze of gin.

'Get your jack over here, Jacko,' I told him bluntly. 'And you with it. There's a fiver up your shirt if you're here in five minutes.'

He crossed the mews so quickly, he hardly had time to put the phone down.

Close to, out of his own background, Jacko looked even worse than when I'd seen him the other day. Yellow eyes were flecked with blood; his breath wheezed like exhaust through a blown muffler.

'A gin. I must have a gin. These bloody stairs are bad for the heart.'

I poured him five fingers of neat gin. His tongue flicked out like an anteater to taste it. Then his eyes moved back a few inches inside his head. I poured him the other hand. Jackson drank that, too. I saw Love watching him with interest. Jackson wouldn't need the undertakers to pickle him when he died, I thought.

'If you want a fiver for two bottles, and you obviously do,' I told him, 'who are these buggers?'

He hadn't even seen the other people on the floor, but now his eyes focused; I could see the irises move like oysters when you squeeze lemon juice on them.

'Can they hear?' he asked.

'Ears have they and hear not,' said Love.

'I hope you're bloody right,' said Jacko. 'The big bloke I don't know. The fellow dressed up as a chauffeur is a strong-arm man.'

'For whom?' I asked.

'People whose names I'd rather not mention.'

'I made a mistake. There are *three* bottles of gin, Jackson, not two. Three bottles, clear as the water you used to make.'

He still shook his head. He had nothing else to shake in his condition. At least, I wouldn't like to see him doing it.

'No,' he said. 'There's enough trouble in my life. But say you run a chain of laundrettes, and one day a fellow comes in and declares he needs like fifty quid a week in notes every Friday to be collected before you shut at seven. And you say, "Piss off". So he does, and nothing happens for a week. Then he calls again, and gets the same message.

'A third week. Then a fellow like this comes in, maybe with a couple of birds, all carrying bundles of washing, say six bundles altogether. They stuff these in six machines and walk out. Each of the bundles contains a couple of pounds of glue; They gum up the machines. Next week, the same thing happens, but with different people, and involving twelve machines, not six. So maybe you decide to pay. That's the kind of world we live in now.'

'You speak for yourself,' said Love. 'This experience hasn't occurred to me in Somerset.'

'Who the hell are you?' asked Jackson, narrowing his eyes in his efforts to refocus them.

'Just a visitor,' said Love.

'Stay that way then. Keep out of these buggers' path.' He turned to me. 'That was three bottles you said?'

'I'll give you a cheque.'

'Cash,' he said.

'Right,' I said. 'If you also find out about this other character.'

'What's his name?'

I prodded the stunt man with my shoe where he had tried to kick me.

'You heard the gentleman,' I said.

'Black,' he said sullenly. 'Robert Black.'

'Then you're a director of Amsterdam's company. Pagoda

Films?'

He nodded. Now why the hell should he beat up Amsterdam? Was there more to their dispute than Amsterdam had said? And did it matter either way? Not to me, I thought. At least, not yet.

'What are you going to do with these characters?' asked Love.

'This.'

I pulled them to the top of the stairs, picked up their legs and tipped them down over their heads. They turned a cartwheel each, and then lay at the bottom for a little while before they crawled away thankfully.

'People like them are always on the giving end of violence,' I said. 'So it's more blessed for them to receive than to give. What brings you here; anyhow, doctor?'

'To see how the gasket's going on. I'd a couple of hours free before dinner, so I thought I'd call.'

'Come any time,' I told him, as the tart told the customer, and we examined George's handiwork. Then we had a few more drinks. At least, Love had a few; I had rather more.

After he had gone, I locked my door and threw both bolts in case Black felt like calling.

I was in bed before I remembered the oil smears on the Rolls engine. I must ask George to be more careful. Or maybe Black or his chauffeur had been taking a quick gander over the stock while I was away to see what they could lift? This seemed probable, but so unimportant that I pushed it out of my mind as quickly as a philandering husband pushes his girl friend out of the back door when he hears his wife at the front.

Within seconds, I was asleep.

CHAPTER FOUR

George and I spent most of the next morning greasing the cars, cleaning plugs and draining the sediment of what seemed like centuries from their petrol tanks.

I also fitted little gadgets I always fix to any vintage car that could attract a thief. This is simply a bit of pipework under the chassis with an auxiliary one-gallon petrol tank. If I have to leave the car parked anywhere, I turn over the hidden, magnetic tap to this tank, so although a thief-or joyrider or anyone else - can start the car, they'll not be able to drive it more than twenty, miles or so. Then, although the fuel gauge can still read 'full' and the sparks be as fat as a barmaid's thighs, they'll stay stuck until I arrive with my key to unlock that hidden tap.

I had just finished when Amsterdam arrived, smooth and plump as a capon in a camel hair coat, his bruises carefully dusted over. Once more the smell of Brut was strong in the land.

'All ready, I see,' he began.

'Getting that way,' I admitted.

'There's been a bit of a change,' he went on.

'For whom?' I asked. 'Like a change of life, or sex?'

'I mean in arrangements. The freighter we are taking out from Luton is going to be packed with cameras and lights and the portable generator, as well as the film crew, and I can't get a second plane. So you'll have to drive to Dover, take the Channel ferry and put the cars on the train to St. Raphael. You'll catch the same ferry from Marseilles, though. Here's where we are staying.'

He handed me a sheet of paper with a name printed on it. Caselle. The Castle, Venaco.

'This means you will have to leave tomorrow morning. Early.'

He peeled off a wad of francs for petrol and food, which I put in my back pocket without counting. Then he glanced round the cars, taking care that no touch of oil should stain his Dacron trousers or his hundred-guinea overcoat, and finally he wafted away up the mews.

I was quite pleased not to be flying. The idea of trusting myself and my working parts to a charter plane so old that it probably had an outside lavatory - because I did not rate Amsterdam as a man who would spend a pound if fifty pence would do - had not been overpoweringly attractive.

But apart from the arguable benefits of flight, this century has other wonders, not least the pace of life, which means that in my story I don't have to fill in all the twiddly bits as I would have had to do had I been writing in an earlier, age.

Then I would have written: *The day of the voyage dawned bright and clear, and I was up early having my cold tub —* although, in point of fact, it was pouring with rain when next morning dawned, and I wasn't up anything or anyone, nor was I having anything or anyone. My face seemed no more than a hundred years old as it looked back at me from the mirror; and I thought, not for the first time, if I was so clever, why wasn't I rich? Why wasn't I like Amsterdam, ordering people around in an overcoat soft as a shaver's bush? Why was I to take two beat-up vehicles to Corsica in order to turn a not particularly quick gain?

And then I thought of all the other poor devils, these worms who masquerade as men, going into their offices from their tiny suburban houses, or their executive-type maisonettes, which would be theirs in twenty-five years' time, if they kept up their mortgage repayments. Compared to them I was lucky-as the man with one ball told the eunuch.

I threw a couple of eggs in the pan, fried them, squeezed an orange, and was ready for whatever the day might bring. In fact, it brought Dr. Love and Victoria at around the same time; eight thirty.

'We are driving to Dover instead of flying from Luton,' I told them. 'I know the way blindfold, so I'll lead. Keep the speed down to about forty on the open road. On the motorway we'll keep in the slow lane unless people on roller skates try to overtake us.'

I dumped my case behind the front seat of the London-Edinburgh, and then squeezed the five hundred pounds in tenners I always carry when abroad, through the lid of a tin on which was painted 'gear oil - heavy viscosity'. You never know how useful cash can be until you haven't got any. Then we set off, Victoria behind me in the Alpine and Love at the rear in his Cord.

We were in Dover by eleven o'clock and, more important, in the Hovercraft bar a few feet over the sea less than an hour later. Ours were the first three cars to be out on the other side, and we simply drove half a mile to the railway yard, where some Frog manoeuvred them on to the open truck that would trundle behind the train through France to St. Raphael.

Again, if I were telling this story fifty years ago, I'd put in a lot of crap about the French undulating fields and Dame Nature's perennial miracle of spring or summer or whatever, but as I'm not, I'll simply say that the trains in France are very civilised and their meals are extremely good; so are their beds. I slept like an old husband with a young wife and only woke up as we came into St Raphael.

A short drive to Nice, then another transfer to a boat. More to eat and drink, and finally the Corsican coast shimmered like a green mirage on the horizon. A handful of skyscrapers squatted around the bay at Ajaccio as though wondering whether to jump into the sea. We had the cars off the ferry in minutes and set off up into the hills before they decided.

Corsica is really one gigantic mountain. No matter where you are, you're always either climbing up or going down, and usually with a solid grey or red wall of rock on one side, and a drop of hundreds of feet on the other.

We crossed bridges without sides and coasted through small villages where old women in black sat on verandahs and watched us, and others where children played in the swirling dust near brown dogs tethered to doorposts. Some children waved to us and we waved back. And all the time the road climbed relentlessly; the altimeter on my dashboard showed we were at five thousand feet before we were through Vizzavona and over the hump of the hills.

The air felt chill, a trailer for the coming winter, although it was Only the end of August. I was still leading, and I noticed that Victoria's Rolls was finding the longer hills heavy going; a lot of water had poured under these mountain bridges since the days of the Alpine trial. Maybe I should have stripped the engine? What the hell, I thought. We had only to drive about for a few days and then we'd be finished with the cars. And after all, I was selling them, not buying.

The Caselle was a cluster of chalets in the centre of a valley. Seen first from the hill top, four or five miles away in Venaco, it looked like a Western stockade; a large, ranch-like centre building with a frond of smoke at its chimney, ringed by smaller huts all made from round stones, the size and shape of rugger' balls, with wood facings. .

As we approached, I saw a few cars with German and French number plates were parked to one side on a flat area marked by large stones. One was a rented Simca. I knew it was rented because in Corsica self-drive-hire cars have their numbers painted on their plates; all other car number plates have raised figures.

We chuntered in alongside them, our bonnets high as their rooftops, cut our engines and climbed out. The air felt clear and cold as iced gin; a cowbell tinkled against the constant roar of the river in the gorge, loud as motorway traffic.

We went into the hotel. A long bar with two sides, the barman in between them, divided the hall. The ceiling was a chequerboard of white and brown sheepskins; on one wall a hog's jaws were clamped around an electric light bulb. The bar was warm and friendly. Amsterdam stood on the far side, and he came round to meet us, a glass of Cap Corse in one hand, a magnificent Montecristo cigar big as a bull's tool in the other.

'So you've got here,' he began, looking at each of us in turn.

He was like those odd characters who poke their heads round the bathroom door early in the morning, when you are staying in a friend's house, and when they see your chin is white with lather, ask stupidly: 'Oh; are you shaving?'

'Yes,' I said. 'No trouble.'

Another man moved out from behind a stone pillar and stood side by side with Amsterdam, looking at us. He was taller and tougher, about thirty-five, just poised on that Indian summer threshold before fitness dissolved into flesh. In another year he'd have a pot on him like a pomegranate, but right now he looked impressive enough. His face was brown as a tin of boot polish and lined like a very old raisin.

'Meet Jean-Paul,' said Amsterdam. 'The best stunt man in the business.'

'Better than Black?' I asked him. A shadow of anger darkened Amsterdam's Levantine face.

'Infinitely. We're waiting for Jean's colleague to arrive from France tomorrow, and then we're ready to go. Jean-Paul lives near here in Corte, the old capital of Corsica. It was very lucky I found him.'

Lucky for who, I thought. Amsterdam? Or Jean-Paul? Maybe for all of us. I didn't care greatly. We signed the little registration cards that the French insist on, and then went out to our rooms.

We each had a stone chalet, reached by paths radiating from the car park like spokes. Love was in the chalet on my left, Victoria on the other side, a little way behind us. Mine had a bathroom, some chairs made out of dark barrels, and whitewashed walls scored with trowel-points to break up their surface. The verandah, at the back overlooked the gorge.

Far beneath me, the river frothed furiously over huge grey boulders. Across the river, the bank soared up into hills, one folded neatly behind the other, peaks lost in cotton-wool cloud, like a painted stage set. Trees and bushes grew right down to the water on that side. There were no birds, and no sign of wild life of any kind. And then, in a clearing, ringed in by dark bushes, I suddenly saw a man, as still as any tree, watching me.

He was smallish and broad-shouldered, and he wore a jacket and trousers with a bandolier of cartridges around his waist.

He held a shotgun across his body. There seemed something vaguely sinister and menacing in his appearance, in the fact that he was there at all, which was ridiculous. The season of *La Chasse* was just beginning. Soon the hills would be dotted with huntsmen aiming at anything that flew or walked on four legs, from pigeons to wild boar, and the air would echo with their shots.

I waved to him to show I'd seen him, but he did not wave back. I looked down at the water again, and then back at the clearing, but the man had gone, as soundlessly and swiftly as the evening shadows moving down the hill towards me.

The roar of the river seemed louder as the darkness deepened and the air chilled and the crickets wound up the.ir clockwork ratchets and began to whir, while the sun, like a giant tail-light in the sky, slid away over the hills and went to bed.

I climbed down the hill through the gorse and thyme and myrtle and stood staring at the river, .already grey with mist, and then at the clearing where the man had been, but I did not see him again. The air was sharp as a saw-edge with woodsmoke from some unseen fire and that indefinable evening smell of the island; spices and the warm scent of maquis, the ubiquitous herb whose name the Corsican resistance fighters in the war had taken as their own.

The sun disappeared suddenly, and in the almost unexpected darkness I heard a crack, crisp as a bone breaking. Unless I was walking on four feet someone was with me. Could it be the man from the far bank? I turned round slowly. A dim figure was standing a few feet away in an opening in the bushes. Victoria.

'What's wrong?' I asked, surprised to see her, and unreasonably glad it was not the hunter.

'Nothing. Should there be?'

'I'm just a pessimist,' I explained. 'Then anything nice that happens always comes as a surprise. What are you doing out here?'

'Same as you. Taking a walk. Thinking.'

I wanted to say, 'What about? Or who?' but it was no concern of mine.

'I don't like this place,' Victoria went on. 'It's eerie.'

'You're a town bird,' I told her. 'Country silence is like country cream-too rich for you.'

But there was something in what she said. The air felt icy, as though it had been frozen first, and then rinsed through deep dark green water. We walked back up the slope to my chalet more quickly than I had walked down.

I was tired, of course. There's always strain in driving a valuable old car; you never know whether some unseen, forgotten pipe will crack or a tiny wire break in a coil winding. Old cars are like old people; they can pass every physical test and yet almost immediately break down, for most serious defects are always unseen.

'Wait a minute,' said Victoria suddenly. She put out her hand and touched my elbow. I'd rather she'd touched me somewhere else, but this was not the time to suggest it.

'That man Jean-Paul,' she said. 'I'm afraid of him.'

'With a face like his, he probably frightens himself,' I agreed. 'As the Marx Brothers say, I never forget a face although in his case, I'm prepared to make an exception.'

'He is a crook,' she said simply. 'I am sure of it.'

'Most of us are crooked to some extent. It's all a question of degree, and I don't mean an M.A., or B.A.'

'You'll find he has a record as long as your arm.'

Well, he might have had something else as long as my arm, which would put him in an unassailable position. I said nothing. I was bored with this conversation. What this girl felt about some character she'd only seen for a few moments, did not interest me. I would rather hear what she felt about me.

'Come and have a drink,' I suggested. I'm a great believer in the therapeutic qualities of alcohol when dialogue runs dry.

Someone had lit the fire at one end of the bar. No other lights were on, so the whole room glowed red as a furnace mouth. Outside, night had painted the windows black. The barman stood polishing glasses.

'Have you seen Dr. Love?' I asked him in my execrable French.

'Monsieur le docteur has gone into Venaco,' he replied in English, 'with Mr. Amsterdam.'

'Let's follow them,' I told Victoria. 'We can have a drink there instead.'

We walked out to the cars. The plateau was now completely dark, save for little lights that glowed among the bushes to mark the tracks leading to the chalets. I opened the passenger door of the Alpine for her.

'Let's go in your car,' she said suddenly. 'I'm tired of driving in that.'

'As you wish,' I said.

We set off, back up the corrugated hairpins into the village, just two layers of houses, one on either side of the road, perched on the almost perpendicular hill. They clung like stone and stucco leeches, their lavatories built on at the back like sentry boxes overhanging the river. We parked by the main cafe on the left, where metal chairs and tables glowed red and orange under the lights, and walked up the road. Love's Cord was parked half on the pavement, near another cafe, hung with adverts for Pernod, Byrrh and Pastis 51.

Love and Amsterdam were sitting inside a brightly lit room with a juke box and a zinc-covered bar. Its yellow walls were covered with fading photographs of local notables: a religious procession; then a wedding group; then two photographs of French cars from the early nineteen-thirties, a Voisin and a Bucciali, that had been taken outside the bar. The same two men were in both pictures.

One was a tall young fellow with his trousers tucked into his socks in the way affected by some motoring bloods of the time. The other was a smaller, older man with a peasant's squeezed-in face. What stood out from the grainy brown and beige print was the size of the young man's hands, resting on the car door. They seemed out of all proportion, like hams with huge fingers grafted on them.

'Locals?' I asked the barman, as I ordered Pernods for Victoria and me.

He nodded.

'Yes,' he agreed.

'Who is he?' I nodded towards the man with big hands.

'A local landowner, monsieur.'

'And the other man?'

'His chauffeur; at that time.'

The barman was not the most talkative man in his profession, and I regretted this. These cars might still be around lying forgotten somewhere under bales of hay in some ancient barn.

It is not so many years since some English farmers used cut-down Phantoms to pull hay wagons; and maybe old cars were similarly regarded here. I would ask around.

'I thought you weren't coming,' Amsterdam began accusingly as we sat down.

'That's what the actress told the bishop,' I said. Nobody laughed.

I ordered more pastis. There is only one thing better than the first drink of the day, and that's the second; which also goes for other things on life's long journey.

'Must keep a clear head for your work tomorrow,' warned Amsterdam, when it was his turn to buy the round. I didn't let him push his luck or his parsimony too far; reluctantly, he set up another drink for me.

'What *is* the work, exactly?' I asked him.

'First, a sequence on a lake near here. I've just decided on it. Very good production value.'

'Where exactly is this lake, then?'

The only lakes in Corsica I had heard of were high in the mountains and would take hours to reach.

'Near Catareggio - tatty sort of resort, fifteen miles from here. I've a couple of speedboats due to arrive tomorrow. There's a buoy going to be moored out in the middle of the Etang and both drivers of the two boats want to pick it up. It's imperative they bring it in. Never mind why - that's the bloody story. Maybe there's something hidden in it — a message, a fiver - what does it matter?'

'Who gets the buoy?' I asked, not caring a damn, so long as I got my money.

'Neither,' said Amsterdam. 'That's the twist. See?'

I didn't see very much. But so long as all this didn't take too long and I was paid for whatever I had to do, what did it matter? You never go broke taking a profit.

'The stunt man due here tomorrow is bringing the boats. He and Jean-Paul have worked together before, apparently, so we should do the whole scene in a day easily. Then on to your car stuff.'

We chatted of this and that, but mostly that, and then a thought struck me, as thoughts sometimes do.

'Where's the rest of the unit?' I asked. 'The director, the crew, the sound people?'

I've hired out old cars for several films, and my experience has always been that so many people and generating cables and lights and microphone booms and heaven knows what else are around, you scarcely know where to put your feet.

'They've been held up,' Amsterdam said, irritation suddenly etching his bland face with wrinkles, so that he looked like a mandarin who had eaten a bad hundred-year-old egg. 'They're due to arrive about three in the morning. Engine trouble. It's a hired plane.'

'Ah!' I said, as though this explained everything. Maybe it did, at that. We finished our drinks and drove back to the Caselle for dinner.

Afterwards, I checked over the cars and removed everything I could, like tools and rugs and maps, for they would have to live in the open; the hotel had no garage. Then I had a bath and crawled into bed and lay listening to the thunder of the river, wondering whether Napoleon had passed this way on his march to Paris so many years before. .

I also thought about Victoria, and wondered whether he had thought about Josephine, and if his thoughts had been the same as mine. I wondered why Victoria thought Jean-Paul was bent and how did she define a crook? She still had not told me. Then I thought about Black, and wondered once more why he had attacked Amsterdam. There must be a reason - a genuine reason, as I say when I seek to explain in adverts why the last owner has sold a car I am also trying to sell; genuine reason for sale. Whoever heard of an un-genuine reason?

When I recalled Amsterdam's own explanation of Black's behaviour, I thought that I had. Perhaps Black was a psycho, and violence was the only means of persuasion he knew. That could also explain why he attacked me. But would that be a *genuine* reason? I was still thinking about this, and the whole dark uncharted areas of the human mind, when sleep tiptoed up behind me.

CHAPTER FIVE

The roar of an outboard engine splintered my dreams and the crackle of its exhaust blew the last cobwebs of sleep from my mind. I crawled out of bed, pushed open the door and looked over the verandah wall.

An old Willys Jeep was parked near the cars with two white speedboats on a trailer. A man in blue jeans and a dirty sweat shirt was revving up one of their engines, a foolish thing to do out of the water, as it could easily overheat. As I watched, he switched off, and climbed back inside the Jeep. Amsterdam came around the other side and they stood talking together, and then the Jeep drove off slowly, the boats bobbing and bumping behind it.

The morning sun winked off their windscreens and began to burn its way up the sky, drying out the mist. The ground was already steaming. It was going to be a hot day.

I went back into the room, shaved, had a slash, brushed my teeth and walked across to the hotel. Amsterdam was halfway through his breakfast, slices of French bread and honey, with a pot of black coffee. I joined him. He looked depressed.

'What's the matter?' I asked.

'Everything,' he replied grumpily. 'First, the camera crew haven't arrived. I had a phone call last night. They're *still* stuck at Luton. Then the other stunt man hasn't turned up, either.'

'The boats are here, at least,' I told him. 'That's something.'

'So what good are boats without drivers? What good are drivers without cameras? All this is costing me money. *Real* money.'

The way he spoke, with anguish in his accent, made me feel he was paying with his own flesh torn off layer by -reluctant layer from his soft flabby frame.

A waitress gave me a hot roll, and I don't mean one in the hay, but one on the plate, and a jug of black coffee. I ate one and drank the other, and felt more like a human being. Amsterdam wiped honey off his mouth with a napkin and looked at me as though seeing me in focus for the first time.

'I've got Jean-Paul, who can drive one boat,' he said slowly. 'Could *you* drive the other?'

'Of course. For a fee.'

'Have you ever driven a speedboat?'

'Often,' I told him. 'And a hard bargain, to boot, or to shoe, if you prefer it. But what's the use of me driving one boat if there's no one to film us?'

'We have to rehearse first,' he replied. 'Then when the crew arrive we can go right on and shoot. We can do a few dummy runs now and time the thing.'

'What was the stunt man to get for the job?' I asked him.

'Fifty a day. Cash.'

'Francs or pounds?'

'Pounds.'

'Give it to me,' I said. 'For that money, I'll row the bloody boat.'

'Well, let's see how you perform,' he said. 'I'll go and rake up Jean-Paul.'

As Amsterdam went out, Love came in.

'The crew hasn't arrived. Nor the other speedboat pilot,' I told him.

Love raised his eyebrows slightly, as though this did not surprise him particularly; or if it surprised him, it did not worry him. But then, there was no reason why it should.

'They were due in this hotel, were they?' he asked.

'Yes,' I said.

'That's very odd,' said Love, pouring himself some of my coffee. 'Because I checked with the receptionist last night, and no bookings had been made.'

'Now that *is* odd,' I agreed. Because it was.

'Perhaps they are booked in somewhere else?'

'There *is* nowhere else. This is the only hotel for miles. Amsterdam says he had a call from them last night and they're still stuck in Luton.'

'Then he must have had the message by telepathy or carrier-pigeon, for no overseas calls came into this hotel last night. I checked that, too.'

'Why?'

'Because I expected a call from that specialist I saw before we left.'

'So you think they're not coming at all?'

'I think nothing,' replied Love. 'One of the benefits of a scientific education is that one does not jump to conclusions. One follows facts.'

'One does,' I agreed, 'and the one fact to follow here seems to be that Amsterdam's trying to make a film without the benefit of cameras or crew.'

'Who said we are going to make a film?' asked Love.

'If we're not, what the hell are we doing here?'

Was this guy Love a nutter or something?

'Ah! Yes,' he said easily. 'Then I feel that possibly Mr. Amsterdam, and the others like him who shelter their true identities behind the names of cities, may not always speak the complete and utter truth.'

'You mean he is *not* going to make a film?'

'You will jump to conclusions, my friend,' said Love reprovingly, pouring out another cup of my coffee.

'It's the only jumping I'm getting on this trip,' I told him. 'In the meantime, Amsterdam has suggested I take over the second stunt man's job of driving the speedboat. He is also going to pay me for it, which must be a good thing.'

'I'll come along and see you in action,' said Love.

We went out. I collected a pair of sun glasses, put back the tools in the two cars and then we set off. Amsterdam was leading, with Jean-Paul in his hired Simca.

After about twelve miles of diabolical Z-bends, many ominously marked with a red and white stick to show where a car had pitched over the side down the hill, we reached Catareggio. Over a cross-roads, the tarmac track petered out amid dirty sand and parked cars. Even the sea looked grey. The beach was littered with plastic bottles, yellowing papers and thrown-away cigarette packets.

In a fibreboard cafe, a handful of people were playing snooker. One looked up as we drove past and I saw his face clearly; he was the small man in both the photographs on the wall of the cafe in Venaco, older now, obviously, but unmistakably the same. I thought I had seen him somewhere else, too; and then I remembered. He was the man with the shotgun I had seen watching me from across the river on the previous evening.

A sad end-of-season air hung about the place; shabby blue tents, a half deflated rubber boat, broken car springs, and patches of grass on the grey sand that looked like hair sprouting through an immensity of dandruff.

Amsterdam drove off this road, past vineyards on the left, eucalyptus trees on the right, and then marsh lands with wild duck rising. Haifa mile out of town, over a narrow bridge without sides, and only Shell oil tins flattened to mark the edge of the road, we turned into an opening in the right-hand hedge. Two sandy tracks, the width of a car axle, led between the mint and myrtle bushes into a clearing on the edge of a lake. A few tired pieces of paper turned handsprings in the wind that blew a faint smell of sewage from the town.

The man in blue jeans had off-loaded both speedboats into the water that stretched, with cliffs on the right and a spur of land on the left, to a distant opening and the sea. The boats bobbed gently beyond an eight-foot stretch of scum and driftwood, their mooring ropes still tied to the trailer.

The clearing was shielded by a half circle of bushes and trees which muted the occasional whir of a car on the road, and the clatter of an out-of-sight tractor. Small waves came trembling into the scum, and emerged on the shore as faint ripples. There was a strange airless oppressiveness about the place, despite the wind, as though we were hemmed in by the woods, and an odd continuing sound, a faint plop and splash in the water. It took me several minutes to realise this was the sound of fish jumping; the lake was alive with them.

'This is it, then,' said Amsterdam, coming up to us. 'There has been an anchorage here since the Romans were in Corsica, so the guide book says.'

'Not too much has happened here since then, either,' said Love, looking around. Apart from our vehicles, the only sign of the twentieth century was a dredger half a mile out in the lake. Unseen sea birds were crying faintly; the fish leapt and fell back in the water again. The man in blue jeans came up to us, wiping the palms of his hands on his jeans.

'Ready when you are,' he told Amsterdam.

Jean-Paul turned to me.

'Ever done anything like this before?' he asked.

'No. But there's always a first time, as the old maid told the poove. What should I know that I don't?'

'First, keep your head down, yes? Then, if the boat goes over, you'll be inside a bubble of air, and you can dive and get out. Remember, if the edge of the screen hits your head, we might as well bury you at sea. You'll be the headless man of Corsica:'

'So what else should I know?'

Clearly, I was going to earn my fifty quid. '

'If there's any aggravation, pull the throttle right back. But always keep the engine running. Speedboat without an engine running is about as much good as a bridegroom without a bride. You can't control it. Weight distribution's all wrong.'

I looked over his shoulder into the nearest boat. It had the usual fibreglass hull with a rev counter, speedometer and temperature gauge on a dashboard in front of the steering wheel. To the right of the nylon seat was the ignition key and starter button, and a lever in a quadrant linked to the throttle.

The farther forward it was pushed, the faster the engine

turned. Pulling it right back engaged reverse. , The engine was a fifty horse Mercury which should give the boat about 45 miles an hour or, if you want to talk in sailor's language, about 39 knots. There was nothing here I couldn't cope with.

Amsterdam tugged the nearest rope. The boats bobbed in towards us gracefully and reluctantly, as though they had a will of their own.

'Keep out from the shore,' he warned both of us, 'because of all this junk floating around. You'll only foul up the propeller. And watch out for driftwood. I don't want any insurance claims.'

'Neither do I,' I said feelingly.

'Follow me out into the middle of the lake,' said Jean-Paul. 'I have a walkie talkie to Mr. Amsterdam. When he tells me to start, I'll raise my hand. We'll weave round in opposite directions in a circle of about a hundred yards, at first.

'When you get the feel of it, we'll narrow this distance until we are passing and re-passing, turning on our ends and so on, always round that buoy.'

'How long does this go on for?' I asked.

'Until you get it right,' replied Amsterdam. 'It will only take up two minutes of screen time, but it may take hours out there.'

This all seemed a bit vague to me, but then filming wasn't my business, and everyone else's business looks odd until you know what it's all about.

If you saw a man spend his whole working life boring tiny holes in box-wood and then stain the wood, and rub dust and mud into it, so that it would look like a worm-eaten piece of antique furniture, carved by Chippendale's mother-in-law or whoever, you might think that's odd, too. But a fellow at the other end of my mews has bought a country house in Sussex, a flat in Chelsea, and a Rolls from me, simply through doing just that. He bores to fortune, as you might say.

'Ready?' asked Amsterdam.

I nodded, took off my shoes and socks, put them side by side on the shore, like the shoes of the fisherman, rolled up my trousers and waded into the water. It felt cold as dry ice. I climbed thankfully over the side of the boat and checked the fuel; three-quarters full. I unscrewed the air-vent nut in the top of the tank and squeezed the rubber bladder to prime the carburettor. Then I turned back to Amsterdam.

'What about a Mae West?' I asked him. Swimming is all very well in the warm Med, but in this freezing water, it was a different thing altogether.

'They should have come with the boats,' he called back, 'but they didn't. You'll have to risk it this time.'

'Where's Jean-Paul?' I asked, for he had suddenly disappeared.

'Gone back to the car. Wants to put on a rubber suit and a diving cap in case he goes over the side.'

'What about me, then?'

I hadn't even a flattie on my head, and felt naked as the leader of a nudist convention.

'You'll be O.K. He's got the tricky bits to do, turning in front of you and so on. You just keep going round in a circle.'

That shouldn't be difficult, I thought. I'd been going round in circles ever since I had agreed to hire out these old cars: at the present rate of progress, I'd keep on in ever diminishing circles until, like the dreaded Oozoo bird, I disappeared up my own jack.

I sat in the bobbing boat, hearing the chuckle and slap of the water on the other side of a quarter inch of fibreglass, and wished I'd never agreed to do this. After all, everyone to his trade, and my trade was on land. I've never been a water baby, and I felt too old to learn.

Then I saw Jean-Paul coming back, taking great strides along the path. He wore a black rubber wet-suit with a yellow stripe down the legs, and a black cap and goggles over his eyes. Amsterdam was shouting something to him that I couldn't hear, and he nodded and raised his right arm in acknowledgement. He pulled himself up over the side of the other boat, primed the carburettor and started his engine. A faint blue haze of exhaust drifted away from the stern.

He perched up on the right gunwale, steering with his left hand, gripping the control lever with his right, and put the boat over in a wide turn. The propeller carved a curved white wash. So much for his advice to me about keeping our heads down, I thought, starting my own engine. We puttered gently out into the middle of the lake.

Jean-Paul was on my left now, about twenty yards away. He waved to me and I glanced back towards Amsterdam. He was standing with Love and the man in blue jeans, watching us.

Ahead, I suddenly saw the marker buoy, a giant red and white top bobbing in the glassy greenish water, and throttled back. It was impossible to hear anything but the crackle of our engines. Jean-Paul gave the thumbs-up sign and I replied in the same way. Then he waved his hand and we both headed out from the buoy. I kept looking backwards, and when he waved again I slowed and turned to the left and waited.

I could just see the buoy; a tiny striped dot on the shimmering surface of the lake. I pushed forward the control lever and leaned on the steering wheel to turn. Just for a second, the boat's weight fought me, and then the hull came over at a forty-five-degree angle, with the water only inches away from my right shoulder. I increased speed gradually. The boat surged forward.

Suddenly, the water was hammering under my feet like a blacksmith gone mad, or an old maid trying to get into a sex-maniac's cell. The windscreen streamed with spray. In order to see at all, I had to sit up on the right gunwale, like Jean-Paul, steering with my left hand, controlling the throttle with my right. The wind was so strong it caught the breath in my throat and made me choke; my eyes, unprotected by goggles, filled with tears.

I was running into my own wash now, and the boat bucked like a seesaw. The whole hull trembled, and then shook itself like a dog. All I could see of the buoy were odd glimpses through the bow wave, and then I saw Jean-Paul in the other boat coming towards me. He was crouched down behind the windscreen now, his head in its rubber cap like a black pellet. He was past in a flash and a great gout of spray swamped over the side, soaking me to the skin. The water swelled heavily from side to side; its weight made the boat feel sluggish.

I glanced down at the speedometer; twenty-five knots.

I increased speed to thirty, which seemed fast enough. We turned in great circles that gradually grew smaller. A haze of spray and blue exhaust smoke hung like a fog over both of us. Now and then I caught a sudden, brief glimpse of the buoy or Jean-Paul's boat and then I was past them and banking to turn.

I glanced at my watch. I'd been going round in a circle for nearly ten minutes, and felt sick as a serpent; I could hardly see the damned buoy, I was so dizzy from the continual circling.

I throttled back and the bows dipped and the boat centred herself, but slowly and wearily, because of the water I had shipped. The wind blew fumes back from the exhaust, making me queasy. Surely we had rehearsed enough? Wasn't Amsterdam satisfied yet, or what?

Suddenly, I saw Jean-Paul coming towards me once more, accelerating all the way. I waved to him to stop. He was still about a hundred yards off, carving an arrowhead of white water out of the heaving glittering lake, travelling so fast that all I could see behind him was a huge plume of spray from his wash, fanning out like the giant tail feathers of some astonishing sea bird.

He was going far faster than either of us had travelled so far; this *must* be the last round before we turned back to the shore. He was barely thirty yards from me when he swerved. And then, instead of passing me by a matter of three or four feet, he came right at me, head on.

I threw my gear into reverse, hard up against its back stop. The shock flung me forward into the windscreen. The boat shuddered and shook like a living thing, and then we ploughed back, water billowing over the stern into the cockpit from the reverse wash. It was already a foot deep, swilling around in a froth, like a boatload of Guinness. Within seconds it swamped the battery. My engine choked and spluttered and died.

I swung the wheel full to the left, but just too late. The bow of Jean-Paul's boat caught mine. I had a sudden instant sight of the strengthening ribs beneath his hull, coated with light green slime. Then my boat rose up under me like the shell of a giant white turtle and blotted out the sky, and I was in the water, shooting down through ever-deepening green, towards the hidden depths of darkness.

I stopped struggling, and held up both arms, hands bent back, until I started to rise. I broke surface and vomited out the water I'd swallowed, gasping for breath. The cold was a vice that squeezed the air from my lungs like toothpaste from a tube. I trod water, sobbing for breath, swallowing, choking, gasping.

Great waves rocked me as though I was in a whirlpool. I was surrounded by a pool of oil, blue and iridescent on the surface of the lake. Twenty yards away bobbed the boat's red petrol tank. Petrol is lighter than water, I remembered, and struck out towards it, and then lay thankfully across it, hardly feeling the sharp handle pressing into my chest, grateful for any floating support as the lake boiled around me.

Gradually, the waves subsided and the ripples smoothed themselves away. I could see the wash of Jean-Paul's boat as it raced on towards the shore. Seconds later, I heard the crash. He had driven the boat right up on the beach. The engine screamed hysterically across the lake, propeller out of the water. Figures were running away from the boat, and then towards it.

Never mind him, I thought. He's ashore. And stunts like this are his business. What about me?

I tried to shout, but my voice had been blown out of my body with my breath. I could only gasp.

I kicked my legs in a crawl stroke and slowly began to move towards the shore. The cold was so great that soon I could not even hold on to the tank. It slithered away, bobbing gently, just beyond my reach or strength. My fingers turned blue and locked like a dead bird's claws, without either grip or movement.

But now I heard the welcome put-put-put of a little boat. Some coracle with a tiny outboard was coming towards me. It circled round and stopped. Two men regarded me gravely, as experts always regard the amateur. I didn't know who they were, but they spoke French. They had a fishing rod in the back of the boat, the hook still baited with a silvery slice of fish. They pulled me in over the side and I lay in my own water, gasping and shivering on the red floorboards, among the mullet and the swilling bilge.

No one said anything. The man. in the stern headed towards the shore. He was chewing an empty pipe, the bowl upside down. His face was brown and lean and honest.

They ran their bows up the beach and cut the engine, and then helped me out. I pulled off my shirt and stood for a minute grateful to the sun for warming my chilled body. I squeezed the water out of my shirt, and used it as a towel.

'Thank you,' I said. *'Merci beaucoup.'*

They nodded, and followed me up the little beach. Jean-Paul's boat was where it had ended its run, a great gout of shingle and grass and earth scored by the outboard.

Jean-Paul lay face down in the space between the two front seats. The boat had several inches of water in the bottom, and this was now streaked red against the white hull. I leaned in and took Jean-Paul's arm, and pulled. He moved heavily, like a sack of meal. His goggles had come off and his face had a surprised look on it, and his eyes were open.

Someone had shot him in the forehead, giving him a third eye just above the bridge of his nose. I let him roll back. I was so surprised myself that I could not hold him.

For this was not Jean-Paul. This was Black, the man who had hit Amsterdam, who had tried to persuade me to change places so that he could come to Corsica.

Well, he had made the journey after all, but he wouldn't be travelling anywhere else, ever.

Amsterdam materialised by my side, a soft slug in.an expensive suit.

Love stood on the other side of the boat, looking down at Black in a professional sort of way. Doctors grow so used to dealing with death, that, like staring up the tails of lovely women in the cause of duty and even getting paid for it, they lose their sequence of priorities. This dead man had tried to ram me. But was this before or after he had been shot?

And who had shot him-and why? And had whoever shot him *meant* to shoot Jean-Paul - or had they known that Black had changed places with him?

'What do you make of it, then?' I asked Love.

'No more than you,' he replied. 'A dead man. A boat at the bottom of the lake. And you lucky to be alive.'

I turned to Amsterdam.

'Before we set off you said you didn't want an insurance claim,' I said. *'Was* the boat insured?'

'Of course. Which means we'll have to go through the motions of getting it out, I suppose. They'll not pay up until they're sure every effort's been made to salvage the boat.'.

'Never mind the boat,' I said. 'What about the man?'

'We can do nothing to help him,' said Love, 'but bits of your boat will keep coming up to the surface. They could sink another boat easily enough. My business is with the living, not the dead, remember.'

'I am remembering,' I told him. 'But let's get this fellow's body out first, before we do any business at all.'

We picked up Black and carried him over to Amsterdam's car, and pushed him into the back seat and then locked the door.

'He'll be all right if you drive slowly,' Love told Amsterdam as he climbed in behind the wheel.

'Where's Jean-Paul?' I asked. The others shrugged; neither seemed to care. Yet surely he must be around somewhere, for he had travelled out from the Caselle in Amsterdam's car? Well, that was his affair, as the husband said when he shot his wife's boy friend in the balls.

'Speaking as a doctor,' Love said gently, 'although not yours, I suggest you get out of those wet clothes as quickly as possible.'

I nodded.

'I'll pay your receptionist as I go out,' I said.

'Just pay me the compliment of having a drink in the Caselle bar as soon as you can.'

There was something about the way he spoke that made me speed back to the hotel, have a hot shower, change and walk over to the bar. Love was drinking a long Glen Grant. I ordered the same; it had more kick in it than pastis. The barman went off to empty ashtrays or polish glasses, or do whatever barmen do when trade is slack. Love glanced round the room to make sure we were alone.

'Ever dealt with Amsterdam before?' he asked.

'No. I'd never even heard of him before he rang me up.'

'You've checked his company, Pagoda Films?'

'In a rudimentary way, yes,' I said, remembering Jacko Jackson and my questions and his answers.

'So you could make another check if you had to?'

'If I had to.'

'You have to. We're supposed to be making a film, yet there's still no sign or smell of a camera or crew. This is costing someone a bomb.'

'You think there's something fishy about it, then?'

'I think nothing,' said Love. 'My profession is concerned with facts. If you come to me with a headache, I don't *think* you've a brain tumour or a cold or eyestrain, unless there are facts to prove it. Maybe you're only wearing your hat too tight. And maybe here I'm just puzzled because I have never been involved in a film before.'

'There is someone I could ring,' I said slowly, thinking of George.

'Well, don't ring from the hotel. Find an outside place. Take one of the cars. Say you've got to fill up with petrol or check the tyres, or something: And let me know the verdict.'

'What about Jean-Paul?' I asked him.

'When he went back to the car to change into his frogman's suit, Black took his place, either with his consent, or without it. If without it, then either Jean-Paul was taken off - which means others are involved — or he's still lying stunned or worse somewhere near the lake. I'll go back and have a gander while you telephone.'

We were just finishing a second whisky when Amsterdam came in.

'Where's the body?' I asked him. Nothing like being basic as the tart said when she dropped her drawers. I hate poncing about with euphemisms about the loved one, or bur late friend, or the dear departed.

'In his room.'

'He was staying here, then?'

'He booked in last night,' said Amsterdam. 'I checked with Reception. There's another thing,' and he looked around conspiratorially to see if we were alone. 'He isn't registered in his own name.'

'What name was he here under?'

'Ravin. With a South African passport.'

'You've been through his stuff, then?' asked Love.

'Of course,' said Amsterdam, as though surprised at the question. 'I thought at first this man Ravin might just be staying in the room. But Black's picture's in his passport. The first question is, who do we see about burying him?'

'We'll try the British Consul,' said Love. 'The next, more difficult question will be, how can you explain his death?'

'It's pretty obvious, I think. One of these French or Corsican nutters banging away at stags or pheasants or rabbits or boar, or whatever they shoot here, must have hit him instead. No doubt, half of them are stoned out of their minds on wine. I'm told it's not safe to walk through a forest here during the season of the chase.'

'It's not safe to go boating, either,' I said with feeling.

Amsterdam turned to Dr. Love.

'Could you help with registering his death? Perhaps, as a doctor, you might be able to organise some French doctor to sign whatever forms are necessary?'

'I'll telephone the Consul this afternoon,' said Love. 'In the meantime, what about your film?'

'We'll have to do this scene elsewhere.'

'If your team are on the way here,' I said, 'won't you wait till they arrive before we try some other lake?'

'I'll tell you tonight. Trying to get a call to London from here is like ringing the moon. There's only one line to the nearest town, and the exchange there speaks no known language. But I'll sort things out. Anyhow,' he added, 'you're not losing, are you?'

'Not our lives,' said Love. 'At least, not so far. Now let's have a closer look at the body. And the passport.'

Black's chalet was the second on the left level with mine, also overlooking the gorge. We didn't knock. The dead are in no position to refuse visitors; they're strangers themselves wherever they are.

Black lay on a tarpaulin which someone had prudently thrown over the quilt so that his rubber suit would not wet the sheets. His eyes were closed, and his face was waxy, the colour of candlegrease, under the patina of death.

Love rolled up one eyelid, examined the finger nails,' pulled down the lower lip to look at the teeth.

'Why are you doing that?' asked Amsterdam.

'To see whether there is any indication of drugs.'

'You don't mean he was drugged?'

'I don't mean anything. But because a man has a bullet hole through his head doesn't necessarily mean it killed him. Just as you may have twenty pound notes in your hand, doesn't mean you are going to give them to me.'

'Too right,' said Amsterdam quickly.

I looked around the room. Black's only luggage was a plastic suitcase. I picked over a couple of Marks & Spencer's shirts, a pair of pants, some socks, an electric razor, a tube of ointment against piles, a toothbrush wrapped in a damp flannel cloth, a South African passport in the name of Emmanuel Ravin.

On the dressing table was a little pyramid of toothpicks and a bottle of anti-dandruff shampoo. It was hard to accept that he wouldn't be needing any of them again. Ever. We all filed out. Amsterdam locked the door behind us and took away the key.

I walked out into the car park and borrowed Amsterdam's car, because it was less conspicuous than mine, and then drove up the hill to Venaco.

In the Post Office I found a *cabine telephonique,* and after some shouting and repeating numbers in English and French, and a wait of nearly half-an-hour, I was through to George.

'I'm in Corsica,' I told him.

'So I hope,' he replied. 'What else is new?'

'I want you to get on to anyone you can at Luton Airport and, using discretion, find out what's happened to the cameras and the crew booked by Pagoda Films to fly out here.'

'They haven't arrived?' asked George in surprise. 'Where can I jellybone you?'

'My hotel,' I said. 'But be careful how you speak. Walls have ears and eyes.'

'Brown Bess - yes. Anything else?'

'Fellow out here got shot in a speedboat. Seems the hunting season's started here. Someone mistook him for a boar. B-O-A-R.'

'One of your lot?'

'Yes. Name of Black. Jacko Jackson knew him. We'd like to know more about him, too.'

'Roger,' said George, which is always a good command, and then the pips went and that was that.

I walked back to the car, climbed in and drove on up the road, with no clear intention of going anywhere, just wanting to be on my own.

I wondered about Black. It was an astonishing accident if some boar hunter's bullet *had* gone wide. But then such accidents did happen.

I glanced at my watch. Three thirty. I began to look for a place to turn the car. The road was very narrow, with a sheer fall on one side to some river, and a mountain soaring up on the left, sheer as a granite wall. It was impossible to risk backing and turning here. I drove on more slowly and then around the next bend, I saw a small hill, capped with blue and red and grey car bodies; a Corsican car wrecker's yard.

Thoughts of discovering some legendary mechanical monster, of buying it at a price absurdly low and selling it at one equally high, surged through my mind. I remembered all the other people who had done this in the past, and I've done it once or twice myself. I drove on more swiftly: I could turn in this yard even if there was nothing to scrounge.

Painted on a wooden board pointing towards a five-bar gate was a notice: *'Carcasses de Voitures'*. Somehow that sounds infinitely more dramatic than the staid signs which appear outside all the English junk yards I know: 'Car spares', and then - 'beware of the dog'.

The gate swung against a heavy spring. I bumped it open and drove up a track cut out of red earth, with a strong wire fence with newly cut stakes on either side. As the road bent and curved, litter grew like some fearful vegetation: empty Omo packets, plastic squeegee bottles, brown cardboard boxes. The track ended on top of the hill in a plateau two or three acres in area, quite invisible from the road far beneath. This was covered with pyramids of rotting refuse.

A dozen fires smouldered lazily like funeral pyres among them, and a swarm of black crows that had been gorging themselves on bones and mouldy loaves of bread, green as corpses, took wing on my arrival.

I stopped the car and then the pyramids moved, changing shape and substance as I watched. They were crawling with pigs and boars, gigantic beasts, bloated and swollen, grouting in the stinking piles; dung eaters and the colour of dung themselves. Their tusks curved like hat pegs out of their slobbering mouths, and as they surged towards my car, their round gross bodies boomed against the metal panels.

I drove on hastily. Some of the beasts started to lumber after me, grunting and sobbing with the unaccustomed exercise, and then they fell back to root amid the steaming mountains of decay. I now realised the significance of the new wire fence which ringed in the whole area. On the far side of it, in the most distant corner, lay the wrecked and abandoned cars. I stopped as close to the wire as I could, jumped out of the Simca quickly and vaulted over the fence. I did not fancy becoming entangled with those tusks.

If you are in the old car business, or even if you vaguely just like old cars, a wrecker's yard can assume the importance of a shrine. All these old cars piled dangerously on top of each other, with doors banging in the wind for journeys that will never now begin, had once been new and loved. Then they had been washed and waxed, and girls had been kissed in them, and men had driven them to important meetings, and sometimes husbands and wives had been uncomfortably but passionately unfaithful in them.

Now these microcosms of dozens of different people, these travelling metal rooms, these extensions of unknown personalities expressed in such individualities as extra chromium strips, two-colour paint jobs, chequered tapes or simply oval STP stickers, and informative advice as 'Sex may be bad for one but it's great for two', were only part of an anonymous heap of tin cadavers in a mechanical graveyard. Lights, instruments, hubs, sometimes even wheels were torn off to fit other, newer cars, as men abandoning one mistress steal back their jewels to give to another.

Most of the cars belonged to the late nineteen-fifties and so were too new to interest me, but here and there, at the base of a mountain of rusting body shells were signs of more interesting remains: a 1927 Citroen lorry, the wooden wheel spokes of an Essex Super Six, a bumper from an old Delahaye coupe.

The dumps of cars had paths of dry grass between them,

where odd axles and smashed battery cases, and here and there a half-shaft or gear train, had been trodden into the earth.

I walked along the first one, hoping to find something worth removing. Then I turned and looked back. Against the barbed wire over which I had jumped a man was standing, a small stocky man with a bandolier around his body and a rifle under his arm. He was the man in the photograph; the man I'd seen on the far bank of the river, and then in the cafe at Catareggio.

There seemed something menacing about him, and yet what could it be? He was only another peasant out shooting, but even so, as I walked back towards him, my hands in my pockets, I kept calculating mentally how far away was the nearest length of exhaust pipe or half-shaft I could use as a club, if it came to fighting. But yet why ever should it?

I walked up to him; I had to if I was to reach my car. The carrion birds were sinking silently down again from the sky behind him to continue their interrupted meal.

Close to, the man's neck was no more wrinkled than the neck of a hundred-year-old tortoise. His face was brown, as though someone had tipped a pot of mahogany stain over it. His eyes were surprisingly green; the cold colour of the sea when the sun goes behind a cloud.

'On holiday?' he asked in English.

'No,' I said. 'Business.'

He nodded sympathetically: some must always work while others play.

'What kind of business, monsieur?'

'My own,' I said, and then, not wanting him to think me rude, for he had a rifle, I added: 'The old car business.'

'Ah. So that is why you are here, yes?'

'Yes.'

'You drove one of those English Rolls up at the hotel - yes?'

'Yes,' I said again.

'They are very beautiful. Tell me, you hope to buy any old cars in Corsica?'

'I live in hope,' I told him, which at least is better than living in debt; or, so they tell me, in sin.

'Do you know of any old cars around here - apart from this junk all round us?' Nothing like coming to the point quickly, as the explorer said when the savage shoved a spear up his jack.

'Yes, monsieur. I do. Two really old cars. French, of course. A Voisin.' He looked at me, eyes flickering like lizards' tongues under his eyebrows to see my reaction. I guessed what the next make would be.

'And a Bucciali.'

So I was right; these two old cars in the photograph were still in the area.

'Near here?'

There is strict etiquette we all observe in attempting to discover the whereabouts, of any antique automobile. You never ask bluntly: 'Where *are* the bloody things?' Any more than, on first meeting a pretty girl, you immediately slip your hand under her sweater. Well not always.

You fence around the subject, showing polite interest, never saying directly that you might be willing to slide your informant a roll of green men for his information. You extract the facts slowly like winkles with a pin. And by winkles, I, mean the sort that live in shells.

'*Very* near,' he said. 'Indeed, only a few minutes in your car.'

'Let's go then,' I said, and jumped through the fence. He climbed over more slowly. I opened the car door. He threw the rifle and the bandolier casually on the back seat.

'My name is Bonheur,' he said. 'Charles Bonheur.'

I told him mine, and climbed in behind the wheel. The pigs and boars rammed us again as we came past the rubbish tip, running alongside, grunting with disappointment when we didn't stop.

'Are they dangerous?' I asked, more for something to say than for an answer.

'Very,' he replied gravely. 'They know the men on the refuse wagon, but they are as good as any watchdog. If they got you down on the ground, then, as you say in England, you have had it.'

'I don't want it,' I said. 'I don't like it that way.'

But I knew what he meant and he didn't mean what I meant. He meant that they would root you and tusk you and worry you, for a hungry pig or a wild boar will eat anything, even a wounded man or a corpse. Especially a wounded man or a corpse.

We drove down the track, out through the gate and up along the road, away from Venaco. Standing in the sunshine had made the car very hot. Heat shimmered in the distance. Down in the valley, by the rushing river, the fir trees stood so near together that an animal could scarcely squeeze between them. And on the other side the cliff soared up, perpendicular as a factory wall.

There wasn't much conversation to make, so we didn't bother to make it. I am never one for clichés that boomerang back and forth between strangers, about how nice the weather is, but we'll pay for it later, and how beautiful the scenery is, and all that crap. Let's get a deal, and then over the hill; that's my philosophy.

After the second or third bend in the road I saw an entrance to a long driveway, overgrown with weeds. Two stone pillars flanked an iron gate, green with moss and wedged open by stones. The nettles grew high as an elephant's alimentary orifice, if there'd been an elephant handy to measure it by. I looked at Bonheur enquiringly. He nodded towards the gateway.

'In here, monsieur,' he said. 'We will park behind the gateway.'

I did so. We climbed out of the car. The air was still as a bank manager's office when you ask for a couple of thousand overdraft without any security.

'Where now?' I asked Bonheur.

'Up the road,' he said.

We walked fifty yards along the road with the smell of myrtle heavy as a perfumery shop. The roar of the river boomed loud as an express train.

Around a corner in the road, on the right, stood a small stone building, like a garage for a desirable detached residence in the 1930s in Esher, Pinner or Penge. But there was no desirable detached residence near it, only this stone building with its slate roof and a rusting iron cross at the apex. Above the door, carved in the stone in black letters were the words, 'Famille Famagusta'.

The doors were as wide as any garage and painted black. Bonheur stopped and I stopped with him. This was obviously a family tomb. He searched in his pocket, pulled out a key half a foot long and opened the door. It looked very dark inside and musty and cool, for no heat could seep through these walls two foot thick.

'What about the cars?' I asked him. 'We can see the corpses later.'

'The cars are in here,' he replied.

I looked at him sharply. Was he a nutter?

I peered behind him into the gloom, and as my eyes grew accustomed to the dimness, for there were no windows, I could make out the outline of an unusual radiator. I walked willingly into the tomb.

The radiator was unusual all right. It belonged to a Voisin, and by its side was a Bucciali, and beyond them again a Renault with a coal skuttle bonnet and a Clover Leaf Citroen, citron yellow with brass door handles and radiator.

I walked round the cars. I did not know what to say, so I didn't say it, but Bonheur did.

'You are wondering why keep these cars in the tomb?' he asked. 'Yes?'

'Yes,' I agreed. 'The thought did cross my mind, just briefly.'

'It dates from the war,' he explained. 'When the Germans came here we knew they would seize everything they could carry away. Some of us, drove our cattle into the hills. Others buried their possessions, even motor cars, in the ground, in quarries and pits, and a few with big family vaults like these, like Monsieur le Vicomte, used them as safes. We knew the Germans would not risk breaking down a family vault because of the hatred this would arouse. They've been here ever since.'

I walked round the Voisin, a car I've heard described as though made by someone who had been told about cars, but who had never actually seen one. It had a twelve-cylinder engine, literally two sixes and linked not in a V formation, but one set behind the other. This elongated engine extended back between the driver and passenger, so that they travelled in what was virtually an enormously long engine on wheels.

The body and the seats were purely ancillary to this gigantic mechanical heart. It was a big ugly brute, with metal panniers on either side of the bonnet for luggage, and an upright, squared-off body. Gabriel Voisin, the designer and builder, had produced aircraft in the First World War, and as a legacy of flight, his car had struts and rods to steady the thin, cycle-type wings. It seemed totally original, even to the blue and gold badge, the Egyptian scarab, the beetle sacred to the sun-god, wings outstretched, symbolising the flight of the soul.

'You like it, yes?' asked Bonheur, watching me.

'It is very rare,' I told him, keeping all enthusiasm out of my voice, as carefully as a publican should keep his water out of his beer. 'Does Monsieur le Vicomte wish to sell it?'

'We will have to see. And what about the other one, eh - the Bucciali?'

That mechanical monument to individuality and craftsmanship, to immense wealth and privilege, and much else that has now all but vanished from our egalitarian world of plastic packages and frozen fish fingers, was also so rare that it was impossible to put a price on it.

This was another monster, with gigantic wheels, each housing a built-in brake drum; with two spares on the rear boot, wearing chromium-plated covers that the years had not tarnished. Along both sides of the bonnet was a chromed likeness of a bird in flight. This Bucciali was a bird I would very much like to persuade to fly in my direction.

To someone who did not understand these things, both could be dismissed as nothing but two mechanical anachronisms. But then you could say the same about the Tower of Pisa by claiming that, because it leaned to one side, its value must be reduced. This, as the song says, ain't necessarily so.

'Is it possible to see Monsieur le Vicomte? Perhaps he might be willing to entertain an offer for them?'

I knew that if I could buy the Voisin and Bucciali at the right price then I was looking at my pension. The only problem was that possibly the Vicomte regarded them as his pension, too.

'We will have to see him in his house,' said Bonheur.

He locked the door again, and we walked back along the road and up the drive. Rhododendrons grew thick and high, and bougainvillea blazed like pink flames on either side of us. Above them towered fir trees, their tops meeting over our heads, making the drive a dark tunnel, dim and hot, where midges buzzed in clouds as though we were entering some land of perpetual evening. The smell of eucalyptus hung thick and sweet as syrup on the air.

The drive must have been the same a hundred, even two hundred years ago. I could imagine gallants riding down it, and the polished iron tyres of carriages striking strong sparks from flints, spotted dalmatians trotting obediently, heads down, beneath the axles. I glanced behind me. Already the gateway showed as a faraway white ring of light. There was still no sign of any house ahead.

'Monsieur le Vicomte is a great landowner,' said Bonheur. 'He owns thousands of hectares.'

'This place seems a bit overgrown?'

'He likes to keep it as it was, monsieur. He is not a man for change, le Vicomte.'

'Does he ever take out those old cars?'

'No, monsieur. Not since the war. He lives quietly.'

That sounded as though he were heavy with gold; I have never yet met a rich man who likes a lot of noise.

'And you are his friend?'

Bonheur smiled, showing teeth yellow as straw, and edged with nicotine. There was suddenly something horrible about his face in the gloom.

'Not a friend, monsieur,' he replied gravely. 'An employee. I work here three days a week. My father was head groom. I was formerly chauffeur.'

I didn't want to ask what Bonheur was now, but whatever it was, he could hardly be the gardener. I had never seen such weeds and thistles: and nettles stood tall as men.

We turned the last bend of the drive and a house loomed up, pinkish walled, with slatted shutters drawn tight-lipped over windows, their grey louvres powdered by the suns of uncounted summers. A terrace, no smaller than a medium airfield, stretched by the front door, and statues, green with lichen, held up huge pots from which creeper tendrils overflowed in green fountains.

Beyond the terrace was a pool; like everything else, overgrown, thickly clogged with weeds and round, saucer-sized water lilies. A bird of some kind took off from a patch of clear water and whackered away on heavy wings.

The front door had a huge padlock on it, new and well-oiled, although the door was old, the paint pocked with burst blisters, the knocker green with verdigris (which is all right for a door knocker, if you like, but not for the knockers I like, which generally go in pairs).

A fish jumped in the pool, and made my heart jump with it. We went up the front steps between nettles and docks and thistles, and Bonheur unlocked the padlock and ushered me into the hall.

I did not know what to expect, so I expected nothing. Even so, I was surprised. The vast hall was empty and uncarpeted. The floorboards were riddled with wormholes, and the fine, dried dust of rat and mice droppings. Stone cornices over two folding doors opening off the hall had crumbled, and a bird that had foolishly flown in and been unable to get out, lay dead at our feet. Rats had eaten its flesh; a flutter of grey feathers and a few pieces of picked bone were all that remained.

A flight of stairs soared up with its marble balustrade heavy and dark with dust, but there was no carpet, and the windows that opened on the landing were shuttered.

There was something about this derelict, crumbling grandeur that made me want to run. It was as though I had strayed into another world only a few hundred yards from the main road; a world beyond time and ordinary measurement. Had I been tricked into visiting this place alone? Had Bonheur followed me from the moment he had first watched me from across the river with this in mind?

I glanced at him. After years of buying and selling you become like an egg-sexer or a policeman; you can tell a baddie right away. There's something about their eyes, their hands, their smile; and Bonheur rang wrong as a cracked bell to me-and yet I had not the slightest proof. It was a feeling in my guts. The sooner I was away, the better for both of us.

'Where's the Vicomte?' I asked him roughly. Surely no one could live in these surroundings, least of all a rich man, who owned this estate?

'I am here,' answered a voice behind us.

I turned, flesh crawling on my back like worms. A man was standing behind the front door. He was tall, and he wore a dark suit with a black silk roll-neck sweater. Both his hands clasped the head of a huge stave. His face was in darkness, but his hands weren't. They were enormous, the giant hands of the other man in the photograph.

'I did not see you,' I explained, and put out my hand to introduce myself. He did not move. I took my hand away. I looked at him more closely, my eyes now accustomed to the dimness.

He was quite blind. Instead of eyes, he had two hollow sockets, dark caverns the size of golf balls, in his skull. His hair was grey, his face cast in a nobility of countenance so that he looked like a stone carving of some grey Greek god.

'I have been looking at your cars,' I told him.

'You like them?'

'Very much. I understand you might be willing to sell them?'

'We cannot discuss business in front of servants,' he replied carefully. 'Everything has its price. In money or in currency of other kinds.'

'True,' I said because it was. But I just wondered in what kind of currency he expected payment.

Bonheur seemed to accept the Vicomte's words as his dismissal. He bowed and held out his hand to me. I had previously folded a hundred-franc note in my trouser pocket until it was no larger than a postage stamp for just this moment; after all, a bribe can be tax deductible. Now I took out this note and transferred it to his palm. His fingers closed expertly over it like a claw, and he was gone. The door closed quietly behind him and I heard the click of his key in the padlock.

So I was locked inside this house with the Vicomte. Why? And, more important, what was going to happen now?

The Vicomte said coldly: 'You were bribing my servant.'

'No, monsieur,' I said hastily. 'Just a small *pourboire* for his kindness for showing me the cars and introducing me to you.'

'I would have made myself known had I *wished* to meet you,' the Vicomte said simply, as though this ended the matter. 'Are you one of these people who think bribes and money can buy anything you wish?'

'Certainly not,' I said hastily, although to be frank and fair, and my name isn't Frank, although I like to be fair, I am; and so, dear reader, are you. Because, believe me, you can always buy anything that is for sale, except for some priceless imponderables like health and eternal life. And when people say smugly that money can't buy happiness, I entirely agree -but would point out that, equally, happiness can't buy money.

'You are,' the Vicomte went on, speaking above my head, and looking away, as though even without eyes he would prefer not to address me directly. 'You are one of the Englishmen at the Caselle. Making some film, so I am told. Some pictorial fantasy for peasants to enjoy for an hour or two, imagining they are in another world.'

'Yes,' I said. 'That would probably describe our activities.'

But would it - could it - when not even a camera had so far arrived?

Suddenly, with a movement so swift I could not anticipate it, the Vicomte whipped up his pole and jabbed me hard in the stomach. I jumped back, almost winded, thinking he had misaimed because of his blindness, and had only meant to make some gesture to emphasise what he was saying. But I was wrong, for he leapt forward pinning me against the wall, with the stick still at my stomach. I felt like a prawn on a tooth-pick.

'You are not there *just* to make a film,' he announced. 'I know. I have had reports. You are there because you seek something in the lake-my lake.'

'Nothing, monsieur le Vicomte. I assure you,' I said, and then I remembered the boat that had sunk. 'All we want to find there is a boat that sank this morning.'

I felt like a little boy who goes next door to ask the disagreeable old lady: 'Please, can I have my ball back?'

'You speak with the accent of truth,' he went on. 'But although *you* may believe what you say, *I* know you do not speak the truth.'

'I don't know what you mean,' I said. 'Bonheur, your servant, or whoever he is, asked if I was interested in old cars. I told him I was, and he invited me to come here. But, maybe, I should leave.'

'You will stay,' said the Vicomte. 'I know something is in that lake. I intend to discover what it is - and why you want it.'

'If you are really making a film, why did you not seek my help? Many other film companies have done so in the past. Do you know that I have the largest collection in Corsica of war-time arms and ammunition, of German and American scout cars, even two tanks? If you are really professional, you would have known this and come to me to seek my help and advice.'

'It isn't that sort of film,' I said. But even as I spoke I suddenly realised that, incredibly, I still did not know what sort of film it was. It could be set in the past, the present or the future in costume, in uniform, or in G strings and fig leaves for all I'd been told. I was glad the Vicomte was blind so that he could not see the puzzlement on my face.

'There was certainly no disrespect intended, Vicomte,' I said carefully. 'I'm only here in charge of the old cars involved, and to drive a boat on the lake. We were rehearsing a scene on the lake this morning and, unfortunately, there was a collision. One of the boats sank.'

'Next, you will tell me it was a fatal accident.'

'Regrettably, it was.' I agreed. 'One of the drivers was shot before his boat crashed. It's the season of the chase. A lot of people are free and easy with triggers.'

'So you, as a mature person, believe that someone in a speedboat can be shot dead through the head by a stray bullet?'

So he knew how Black had died; but I hadn't told him where he was shot. I wondered how much else he knew - how much more than I knew myself.

'It's a thousand to one chance,' I agreed. 'But it has happened before, and it happened here. I was there. In the other boat. What do *you* think is in the lake, apart from fish and water, and the boat we hope to salvage today?'

The Vicomte did not answer immediately, but he withdrew his stick and jammed it on the floor. It had a sharp metal point, so that it stood upright like an instantly planted tree, while he smoothed down his hair with his hands. I moved cautiously to one side. I had a sudden thought of these huge fingers, like bananas with nails, gripping my throat.

'Do not try to run away,' he warned. 'You cannot leave the house in any case. All the doors and windows are locked, for day and night are exactly the same to me.

'There's an airplane down in the lake. I know that. But I don't know whose it is, or who was flying it, or what it contained.'

'How do you know?'

'Because I brought it down.'

'What do you mean-you brought it down?' I asked. My voice was dry now, despite the pastis; dry from the dust of the journey, and the dust of the house. And dry also from another cause altogether - fear. This man was mad; I was deep in nutter country.

'Exactly what I say, Englishman. When you live alone as I do, and when you are blind, you need other eyes to see intruders, to guard your property, to control and preserve your rights. When you walked up my drive, you might have thought that my estate is a jungle, that people could come and go at will, if they so wished, and all unknown to me. But you would be wrong.

'I have no need now of fences, or brick walls. I have electronic devices that show up movements on screens that my servants watch. Other sensors ring bells or alarms that I can hear, so that action can be taken.

'One night, about two weeks ago, I was out on a balcony on an upper floor, when I heard a plane approaching. The engine was too light for an airliner, and no one had sought permission to fly over my land. So he was a trespasser in the sky, just as much as if he were trespassing on my land. So I brought him down. In my vast collection of arms, I have some small missiles that fly blind, that can lock on the heat of an engine in the sky, and follow it no matter how the pilot may try to avoid it, as a shark follows its prey.

'I have to protect my rights, and as a rich man I can afford to do so.'

What kind of a bent-up world had I wandered into here?

'You mean you personally shot down a plane with a missile?' I asked.

'That is so. It crashed in the lake.'

'What about the owner of the plane?'

'What *about* the owner of the plane, indeed? I am most interested to know who the owner of that plane might be. The villagers would not say anything. It was night, and possibly no one saw it fall. Even if they did, a word from Bonheur would persuade them that it was nothing to do with them, and they would forget about it.

'After all, this is a humble community. I own their homes, and their land. My family has controlled their families for generations. I have obligations to them and they know their obligations to me.

'They would keep silence on anything until I gave them permission to speak. And, as you know, they, have kept silence, otherwise you would have heard of this plane. If, of course, you did not already know of it.'

'This is the first I've heard of it. Was the pilot killed? Who was with him? Was it a passenger plane?'

'I am expecting to hear this information from you,' said the Vicomte.

'Then I fear your expectations will not materialise, Vicomte. I know nothing about any plane. I deal in old cars.'

I didn't add, because it seemed unwise, that I felt like someone involved with a car-full of elderly shoemakers - a load of old cobblers - and I would very much like to uninvolve myself. But it was too late now to back out, as the bishop told the choirboy.

'I perceive that you are either a stubborn man or a foolish one,' said the Vicomte sadly, but without surprise, rather as though he had expected me to suffer from either or both of these disabilities. 'Well, we will have to wait until you decide to tell me what I seek to know. You will stay here until you change your mind.'

'A prisoner?'

'If you put it that way, yes.'

I did put it that way. I looked at this man, which was something he couldn't do to me, and I thought: Hullo, hullo, hullo, as the policeman greeted the three-headed man. You're mad. A poached egg. A third division Napoleon, who should be in a steam-room with his hands in those jackets which have sleeves joined at each, end in case he throttled himself. Not that this realisation helped me in any way whatever. But clearly, unless my life insurance was going to have a claim on it, but not by me, the quicker I left the better.

My best hope of achieving this seemed in humouring him.

'Those cars,' I said. 'Could I just have a look at them again . . .'

'No!' He seized my arm with a grip that stopped just short of breaking a bone. His hand was as strong as an Edwardian vice - and not the vice you are thinking of, but the sort they fixed on their solid work benches in their heated motor-houses.

'Tell me, what *was* in that plane, and who was flying it?'

'I have absolutely no idea,' I said. 'Now, if you will kindly take your hand away, we can examine these cars in a civilised manner. Outside, I have something you might like to' - I almost said, 'see', but switched the word in time to 'consider'.

I had nothing outside, of course, except the prospect of freedom.

'You will stay here until you tell me,' he replied, ignoring my suggestion. 'If need be I will beat you until you speak.'

Some people may like this sort of talk, and in Soho the market rate can be as high as two pounds a stroke, but this wasn't my thing, although it could easily be his.

To show he could put his muscles where his mouth was, the Vicomte slowly brought up his stick as he spoke and swung it down sharply on my left shoulder. The stick didn't crack, but for an instant I thought my shoulder blade had. I staggered from the sheer unexpected pain of the blow.

He swung the stick a second time in a scything motion, but because I was down on my hands and knees, he missed my face. He paused, head on one side, like an animal listening for its prey.

'There's no way out,' he said at last. 'No way. If you run, I will follow you through the house and listen for your breathing. And I will keep on hitting you until you speak. How long you stay is entirely up to you.'

My mind began to whirl like the blades of the Schwitzer-Cummins blower on Love's Cord. How the hell *could* I get out, if all the doors and windows were locked from the outside? This lunatic obviously knew his way around every foot of the house, whereas I had never been in the place before, and was hampered by the dark.

In stories I used to read as a boy, in *The Hotspur* and *The Wizard* and so forth, when the hero would be in some incredible situation, such as down a hundred-foot well with water rising, hung with chains round his ankles and wrists, and a ten-ton iron lid on the top of the well, he' would sometimes feel hair prickle on the back of his neck while he brooded on a means of escape.

I have never had this experience before, but I was having it now, for I realised that this man was not joking. He intended to do just what he said. He wasn't making threats, he was making promises. My mind felt like a half-thawed fish finger, soggy and useless.

Ideas of finding instant escape routes, like secret passages, or cellars of the kind one is told used to link convents and monasteries, flashed through it and out again, quicker than Speedy Gonzales could ever flash anything of his.

I stood up cautiously and backed away from the Vicomte until I reached the stairs. Then I began to climb, holding my breath in the hope that this made me more difficult to detect.

'There's no way out to the roof,' the Vicomte called immediately. 'No way at all.'

I didn't argue. He should know; he lived here. Even so, maybe I could hide or barricade myself into one of the rooms, and break down a window shutter and shout for help.

He did not even bother to follow me up the stairs, but stood at the bottom, head half turned, to hear my movements more clearly. He put his stick under his right arm and delved in his pocket and brought out a cigar case and a silver lighter. Then he selected a cigar, after running his fingers over them all gently, and lit it, and waited, puffing contentedly. He seemed to be enjoying himself.

I counted the steps as I went up; forty. It was a tall house. I crossed a landing no larger than the Dorchester Hotel ballroom, and went into the first room with the door open. There was a double bed in the far corner with a big radio set on a cane chair by it, some bottles of Perrier water on a side table and a wash basin without a mirror. Of course; a blind man would never need a mirror.

A strip of carpet was beside the bed, an easy chair, and that was all.

There was nothing I could use as a weapon except the club-shaped Perrier bottles, so I scooped up one in my hand, knocked off the cap, drank greedily, and stood for a second, trying to decide what to do.

The shutters were closed. The only light filtered down through a glass skylight about a hundred feet up in the roof of the house, which was built with a central well from the top ceiling to the hall floor.

I heard footsteps now on the stairs beneath me, slow, steady, relentless as the tread of Father Time. I finished the Perrier, picked up another full bottle and I went up to the next floor. Here, two doors were locked, and the third was open. It led into an empty room where a weary bird, the size of a rook, flapped feeble wings against the filthy cobwebbed window.

The footsteps grew louder; this was not a time to stay. I ran on up to the top storey. There was nowhere else I could go now except down. I was as much trapped up here as if I were in a cellar. The landing was the same size as the others, but the doors of the rooms were smaller; they had obviously been used for servants.

I peered over the balustrade, thick with dust, spattered by bird droppings. I could not see anybody, yet I could still hear feet coming up the stairs. But now others had joined the first climber; he was no longer on his own.

I waited. Around the first landing far beneath I saw the Vicomte. One pace behind him, on either side, walked two other men, black as oiled ebony, wearing jeans and blue T-shirts, their rubber-soled shoes squeaking slightly on the steps."

The man on the left held a two-foot spanner, and the one on the right a pistol. They saw me at the same time as I saw them, and they stopped. They were grinning, and all three looked up at me, although only two could see.

'We are coming for you, Englishman,' said the Vicomte. 'If you will not tell me the truth voluntarily, then my friends here will persuade you.'

He paused for a moment. I stared down at them, sick with horror. There was no way out, no hope of rescue or escape. And I had nothing except the bottle I could throw at them.

'I don't know anything about your plane,' I shouted: 'If I did, I'd tell you, believe me.'

'We cannot believe you,' said the Vicomte. 'You are lying.'

The last word echoed round the stone walls. Lying... Lying...

They began to climb the stairs again. Two more flights. Eighty steps. And after that I doubted whether even the local choir would want me as an alto.

I jumped back from the balustrade. Every second meant that they were a step nearer, yet my brain still seemed numb, as in a nightmare I sometimes have when creditors close in: I am wading through a shallow sea to shore, and a huge green wave is chasing me, to engulf me.

I opened the nearest door. It led into an empty attic with a gurgling water tank walled in by dusty boards. No hope here unless I could dissolve myself like a Disprin and disappear up one of the pipes; and, believe me, the proposition had attractions.

The second door was locked, so I kicked it in; this was no time to hang about. The room behind it was small, the air heavy with the cold smell of oiled metal. Ancient machine-guns on tripods were piled one above the other, with muskets coated with grease, and wooden ammunition boxes. Some were newer than the others and had rope handles, and Chinese characters (letters, I mean, not people) burned into the pale rough wood.

Maybe the Vicomte was in the chop suey business or doing a bit of exporting to the land of the slit-eyed Tong? I opened the nearest box. It was full of wood shavings. I delved down inside and broke two finger nails. I searched around and pulled out a weapon, smaller than a rifle, yet larger than a Tommy gun, with crude sights of cross wires, and a strange-sized barrel about two inches across.

I rammed a bit more and pulled out a khaki metal cylinder with four crude fins spot-welded to its base. The cylinder fitted into the barrel.

What the hell was this? I thought. Then I remembered. The Vicomte had said he had brought down a plane with a missile. This could be a portable missile of the type the Chinese had supplied to North Vietnam to use against American helicopters. Heat from an engine, even from a glowing cigarette, attracted them like a magnet through miles of sky.

I pushed the cylinder down into the barrel and cocked the bolt. I had no idea how the thing worked, or if it worked, but it might frighten the men on the stairs for a moment. And in my state, every minute I stayed alive was a bonus.

I ran out on to the landing. They were now one flight beneath me, and from where I stood I could only see their feet: I shouted. They stopped climbing and leaned out over the balustrade and looked up at me. I kept the weapon behind me. When they came close enough I would use it as a club. It was three to one, but at least I should make a mess of one of them, which would reduce the odds to two to one which, from my point of view, must be a good thing.

The Vicomte's cigar glowed red as he drew in his breath, wondering what I was doing.

I could see his face, varnished with sweat from the climb, the holes in his head where his eyes had been, deeper and darker against his pale glistening flesh. His two companions stood grinning at me. Their teeth, unnaturally white in their faces, reminded me horribly of tombstones. But would they be theirs or mine?

'Do you want to tell us the truth yet, Englishman?' asked the Vicomte.

'Yes! I'll tell you the truth!' I shouted back. 'You're bloody mad! Insane! You should be in a home!'

My left hand tightened on the neck of the Perrier bottle. I' shook it vigorously to arouse the gas in the water, and then flung it down towards the three men.

It missed them all.

I am a bad thrower - I never made any cricket team at school - and the bottle hit the step at their feet. The Vicomte gave a great cry of alarm as it exploded like a bomb. His hands went up to his face and I saw blood run out between his fingers, where splinters of glass had cut him.

The negro fired his pistol. He also missed me, but not by very much. His bullet scored the marble edge of the balustrade. I jumped back, bringing the strange rifle I had found up across my body, and he fired again.

This time, his bullet hit the barrel and the shock of the impact almost knocked it out of my hands.

My muscles tightened against the sudden jerk and, in a reflex action, I squeezed the trigger. The gun went off with a fat soft bang and a heavy sluggish recoil.

The strange projectile I had stuffed down the barrel flew up like some splendid four-tailed bird. It soared away, out through the skylight, showering us all with jagged strips of glass as the window shattered.

The three men jumped to one side to avoid them and the negro fired again. His bullet tore a thin furrow of plaster from the wall behind me. I backed into the open door of the attic, and as I moved I heard a roar above me like an oxyacetylene welding torch.

I looked up and saw the missile stream back through the skylight. Its engine had started and it had turned in the air. Now it shrieked wildly past me, trailing a tail of yellow flame.

Then, as though with a mind of its own, it suddenly changed direction, and flaring like a giant firework, streaked straight down the centre well towards the three men.

The two negroes jumped to one side and pushed the Vicomte down on his face, but his cigar was still clamped in his lips. The weight and impetus of the missile carried it on past them, and then again, as though with second thoughts, it turned in a big circle, spurting flame edged with black smoke, and homed in on his blind, blood-spattered face.

The heat of his cigar had apparently activated the missile's infra-red guidance system. For a second it lay against his face like some strange metal pineapple, while his hands groped madly for it against the fountain of flame that flowed from its tail. Then it exploded.

The force of the blast flung me back against the wall. I hit my head and slid to the ground, all breath blown from my body. There seemed no air left to breathe, only a terrible stench of burning flesh, and the hot, dry bitterness of some unknown explosive. I heard screaming, and then I heard nothing but the roar of flames, like the mouth of a blast furnace.

I crawled to the edge of the landing and peered down. The whole well was filled with flame, white at the centre, yellow at the tips, flecked with thick smoke, from the three burning bodies.

It was impossible to escape down there past this inferno. And yet how could I escape, where I was?

I reeled into the attic again, sobbing for breath. My suit was covered with grey dust, my eyebrows and hair singed, and the inside of my nose and throat felt rough and burned, as though I had been breathing deeply at the open exhaust of a straight eight Packard.

I could see a fireplace across the room, with an old iron dog-grate. It must have a chimney, and surely a chimney meant a way out?

I crawled into the fireplace and peered up, desperate for freedom and fresh air. Twenty feet above me I saw blue sky through the blackened square frame of the stack.

Bricks had been let into the walls of the chimney. As in England a hundred years ago, no doubt little Corsican boys had been sent up with brushes in their hands to clean out the soot and the birds' nests. Well, where they could go, I could go also, or at least I would have a bloody good try.

I stretched out my hands to the nearest two bricks and pulled myself up until I found a foothold against the walls. Then I began to climb.

I went on climbing until my head and shoulders were out of the grey stone chimney. I put my elbows over the edge, and hung there thankfully like a toad, half in its hole, half out, eyes blinking in the unexpected and welcome brilliance of sunshine.

Far beneath me wisps of smoke were growing from gaps in shutters. I heard a crash faintly and far away, as the staircase fell, and a shower of sparks spurted up through a further set of chimneys. Now flames pushed out their orange tongues boldly through the slats of shutters, and the paint blistered and turned black and then the wood caught light. This was no place to linger, as the lodger said when he heard the landlady's husband coming up the stairs.

I hauled myself out on to the chimney and slid down gingerly until I sat astraddle the roof, one leg on either side.

Then I saw Bonheur, standing on the edge of the trees, and shouted to him; he was just the man to help me quickly; he would know where there was a ladder.

'Get help!' I yelled. *'J'essaie de descendre!'*

It might not have been good grammar, but it made good sense to me.

But Bonheur said nothing, nor did he move towards me or anywhere else. Instead, he reached behind a tree and brought out his rifle. What was he doing that for?

Then, as he loaded, I realised. The bugger was going to shoot me as I sat there, split-arsed on the roof. He wouldn't shoot a sitting bird; that would not be sporting. But I wasn't a bird; I was a stranger, an interloper, and therefore an enemy.

The feeling I'd had earlier that he had lured me here had been right; I had escaped one trap only to fall into another. Even as I watched in petrified amazement, he raised the rifle to his shoulder and took aim.

His first shot lifted a tile just ahead of where I was sitting. It splintered into red slivers. Three inches nearer, and that bullet would have lifted my manhood and taken it away for ever.

I braced my back flat against the chimney, anxious for any cover I could find. Bonheur lowered his rifle, blew down the barrel. Then he reloaded, and fired again. This bullet blew the right heel off my shoe. I pulled up my foot to make his target as small as possible. Obviously, now that he had the range he could pick me off easily, and he intended to - but only after he had ringed me round, just to show how good he was.

'Stop firing!' I shouted down to him. Maybe I could do a deal with him; I didn't know what, exactly, but anything would be better than dying like this.

He paid no attention to me, but raised his rifle for the third time. Then he lowered it, and put up his left hand to his right eye to wipe away some fleck of burning ash that the wind had blown into it.

I stretched my hands out behind me and felt the roughness of the chimney. The bricks were so old that they crumbled like warm dust under my frantic fingers. My only hope of survival when Bonheur fired again, whether he hit me or not, was to pretend to be hit mortally, and to fall back as though I was dead, and trust he would not fire again. But first I had to make sure that the chimney would not collapse under my weight. It seemed firm enough.

I glanced down at him. He was raising his rifle again, very slowly and deliberately, enjoying the situation. I took a deep breath, tensing my muscles as though this alone could keep the bullet out of my body.

I imagined it plunging red-hot through pink, splintered bone, through living tissue and sinew, through flesh. My flesh. Then, as Bonheur pulled the butt into his shoulder, I saw a faint movement in the foliage behind him. A man in a grey dacron suit was standing less than a yard away - and Bonheur had not seen him.

Bonheur moved his rifle slowly to select the best bead on my body, and in that second the man jumped on his back.

He jammed one knee in the small of Bonheur's back and as his right forearm went under his chin, like a meat hook, he plunged his left hand down into Bonheur's crotch with a vigour that I would have been pushed to exceed had I been there, although I would have done my best. Bonheur collapsed like a question mark folding up.

Dr. Love picked up the rifle and shouted up at me.

'What are you doing up there? Sunbathing?'

'You've saved my life!' I shouted back, weak with relief. A cliché, but true, as most clichés are.

'And you're not even a patient! How are you going to get down?'

'I don't know.'

I didn't greatly care. Relief swept over me in a great warm tide, rich as the bedtime cups of cocoa my mother used to make. I was alive, and the sun was warm, and who knows, I *still* might be able to buy those old cars cheaply.

Adrenalin poured thankfully through my veins again. I grinned in a stupid fashion, and at that moment I heard the wail of sirens and the local fire engine crashed up the drive through the trees, its ladder breaking the overhanging branches like matches.

Corsicans in grey and blue uniforms jumped down and began shouting about watercocks or other cocks, while colleagues ran out the ladder. It only reached as far as the gutter, but that was good enough for me. I swung my leg over the roof, hung on to the rim by my fingers and then, with the sides of my feet splayed out, slid down the mossy tiles until I felt the edge of the gutter firm beneath me. Then my feet were on the rungs and I was climbing down, hand over hand.

Love was waiting at the bottom. He held out a silver hip flask of Glen Grant. I drank it in one swallow.

'What happened?' he asked, putting the empty flask back in his pocket.

'I'll tell you later,' I replied. 'I don't know how many of these locals understand English. How did you get here, anyhow?'

'My usual form of locomotion - car and foot,' he replied. 'I drove into Corte, saw the consul about Black and arranged for an undertaker to collect his body. I then, had a pernod, a quick look round the town, and was driving back when I saw the Simca parked in the gateway and flames and smoke over the top of the trees.

'I also saw a number of locals running about, and I asked what was happening. They said some blind man lived here, a squire or something, and so I turned to see if I could help either you or him. Where is he, by the way?'

'Dead inside,' I said. 'I hope.'

'The fire killed him?'

'In a sense.'

'You'll have' to explain why you were on the roof,' said Love.

'Gladly. I couldn't get downstairs because of the flames, so I climbed out to try and attract attention. By the way, where's that bastard Bonheur who was trying to shoot me?'

'Behind us, in the bushes. He'll be quiet for a while.'

'I want to be around when he wakes up,' I said grimly.

A Corsican wearing a blue uniform, with a couple of days' growth of beard and breath like a chimney in a garlic factory, climbed out of an official blue van that had just arrived. Some of the firemen nodded towards me. He crossed over, and I made a vague gesture of salutation.

'You are English?' he asked in English.

'Yes,' I said.

'I understand you were on the roof. What were you doing there? Are you a trespasser?'

'No,' I said. 'I was invited to visit Monsieur le Vicomte. I am interested in vintage cars and someone brought me here to meet him.'

'Who?'

'Charles Bonheur. He introduced us, and then left us alone.'

'And then?'

'Well, this man Bonheur locked me in the house. The Vicomte seemed a very-ah-hospitable man.'

'Hospitable! What did he give you, that you should describe him so generously?'

'Well, nothing, really. Not actually *gave* me anything.' Except, I thought, but did not say, a blow on my shoulder and a prod in my guts with his stick. And a bit of climbing practice on the roof after I'd shot three men with a missile I'd never seen before. Altogether, the Vicomte had given me the chance to do a lot of things I hoped I'd never do again.

'He has never given *anything* to my knowledge to anyone. Nor his father before him. Nor his father's father before that. He was mad. A bastard!'

He spat on the ground.

'But he was rich, monsieur. He controlled much of the northern part of the island. And with no eyes himself he bought the eyes of others. He used informers, and every kind of gadget to catch people poaching or trespassing or even just camping on his land. So what did he give you?'

I thought of saying, honestly, the fright of my life. But I said nothing and just shrugged.

'We discussed cars,' I said. 'He took me upstairs and somehow the house caught fire beneath us. He plunged down in the flames. I didn't see him again.'

'Was he alone?'

'At the beginning, yes. Later, two others joined us. Dark-skinned gentlemen.'

'Ah, yes,' he said. 'I know them. Or rather, I knew of them. North Africans. But no one could live in that inferno.'

He looked at the house, blazing now like a huge stone torch. Giant flames poked long tongues at us from the windows. The shutters had long since been burned away, and the glass in the windows had melted. The heat was so strong that branches on the nearer trees were crackling like Yule logs.

The firemen were valiantly pumping in two or three wavering jets of water from the pond. They boiled and burst into steam as they hit the baking walls, but for all the good they were doing they might have been peeing on the place.

'They must all have perished,' said the fireman, and he made the sign of the cross. At that moment, I heard a faint, furtive movement, like an animal in the bushes, and saw Bonheur beginning to run. I charged after him through the undergrowth, but he knew the secret paths between the creepers and the tangled trees, and was away. I stopped and heard the, crash of twigs and branches grow fainter as he increased the distance between us. I turned back slowly towards the house.

'Where are you staying, gentlemen?' the Corsican asked.

'The Caselle.'

'Someone will take a statement from you there, then. It's only a formality, you know. You are tourists?'

'No. We are working here. On a film.'

'Ah, I see. You have pretty girls with you - yes?'

'We live in hope,' I told him.

The fireman nodded.

'Yes, always we live in hope. And even without hope, we live. Until, one day, something like this happens and then there is no hope.'

He shook us by the hand again and walked over to his men.

CHAPTER SIX

I didn't entirely agree about the hope thing. I was just living, but that was enough for me. Love and I walked along the drive to our cars.

'Now what *really* happened?' he asked me when we were on our own.

I told him.

'So he was a nutter, this Vicomte?'

'I would not disagree with that description,' I admitted. 'But a rich one, and powerful. He obviously *had* brought down some plane that had offended his sense of territorial rights by flying over his land. And he knew it had crashed in the lake, or he wouldn't have thought we had something to do with it.'

'Have we?' asked Love.

'Not me,' I said. 'I'd never even heard of the damn thing.'

'Nor me. But that doesn't mean that Black was or Amsterdam is as ignorant as we are.'

'But how has no one missed the plane? And why did no one see it come down?'

'Probably the owner *has* missed it - unless he died in the crash.'

'Do you think this whole filming is just a cover for something else?'

'As I've already told you, I don't like *thinking* anything. But rehearsing a sequence on a lake, when one boat sinks and will have to be dredged out, *could* provide a very convenient cloak to dive in the water - and the chance to see who or what is in that plane.'

We drove back to the hotel. The receptionist came out to meet us as we parked the cars, wringing his hands as though washing them without water.

'Ah, monsieur le docteur,' he said to Love, 'Mr. Amsterdam was asking, would you please go to his room immediately?'

Amsterdam was in his chalet, shouting into his telephone as though by sheer volume he could overcome all defects in local exchanges, poor connections and even distance itself.

He banged down the instrument, poured himself a glass of mineral water and looked at us in some irritation. I felt like a schoolboy up in front of a master enquiring into certain goings-on behind the bike sheds.

'Where have you been?' he asked Love. Then, turning to me: 'And what happened to you?'

'You know damn well where I've been,' said Love. 'You asked me to register Black's death.'

'That wouldn't take this long,' interrupted Amsterdam.

'It didn't,' agreed Love. 'I was on my way back when I saw your car parked outside a house on fire. I stopped and found *him* there.'

'What the hell were you doing? Are you a bloody pyrotechnic or something?' Amsterdam asked me sharply.

'Something,' I said, and gave him a bare outline of my experience.

'*Everything's* gone wrong,' went on Amsterdam, hardly listening to me. He pressed his palms into his eyes as though to hold back tears. '

'First of all, we lose a boat. I've been on to Bastia - there isn't another we can hire. And now the insurance people are complaining we haven't made enough attempts to salvage the bloody thing. They're coming over later today to have a go themselves.

'Then this fellow Black - I'd no idea he was even out here - goes and gets himself shot. What if he has a wife and family who put the legal button on me? They say any publicity's good publicity so long as they spell your name right. But not this. This whole venture has a jinx on it.'

'Balls,' I said'. 'People put jinxes on things themselves. And my view is that you have not been quite as frank with us as you would be, were we talking in different circumstances.'

'Like what circumstances?'

'Like me with one hand gripping your bollocks and the other at your throat,' I said. 'Don't give me all this crap about jinx on your film. I don't believe there *is* a film, or there ever was one. We haven't seen a camera, a technician, not even a bloody actor, since we've got here.'

'I've just been on to London, telling them not to come,' he said. 'You heard me.'

Love picked up the telephone, looking at Amsterdam as a biologist with a microscope might examine some new amoeba that had somehow strayed on to his slide.-

'Quel numero vous voulez.' asked the operator.

'None,' he replied in French. 'Only to find out what number Mr. Amsterdam was speaking to in London just now.'

There was a pause. I could hear the faint rustle of paper as the girl scanned through her notebook.

'Monsieur,' she replied, and we all heard her voice clearly. 'He was not connected to anybody. He was just *speaking* into the telephone.'

'Thank you,' said Love.

'You see,' he continued, still looking at Amsterdam. 'You're the only actor we've seen here. You picked up that phone when you heard us coming up the stairs.'

'You're like the joke tycoon who's always on the blower to Rome and Venice and L.A., and actually it's only the typist who's ringing from the office next door,' I added.

'You're not here to film at all. You're here because a plane came down in that lake two weeks ago - and you want to know who or what was in it.'

'You must be mad,' said Amsterdam slowly, looking at me in amazement, his mouth open. But was he amazed at this suggestion - or that I had made it?

I could imagine his brain turning uneasily in his head like a sleeper in a railway couchette after a hot lobster supper. He glanced at Love and then back to me. What kind of people was he surrounding himself with? How much did we know-or did he think we knew?

'I don't know what you are talking about,' he said at last, with some dignity. 'We seem to be on entirely different wavelengths.

'I hired you two gentlemen to drive out two vintage cars I wished to feature in a film. We've had bad luck, which surely even you do not seek to deny. Now you accuse me of being involved in some incident or accident I've never heard of — and not even telephoning London when you actually came into the middle of my conversation.

'It is clear we cannot continue to operate together in these circumstances. I suggest, therefore, that we cut our losses. Instead of trying a new location, we drive back to Ajaccio, catch the earliest ferry back to Marseilles, and then go home to England. I will then make other arrangements for the whole enterprise. I had intended moving to another location, but without goodwill, there is simply no point.'

I picked up the telephone.

'When is the next ferry from Ajaccio?' I asked the girl.

'One leaves at nine o'clock this evening, but it is fully booked. The first with any vacancies sails at six in the morning, the day after tomorrow.'

'Book our three cars on it,' I told her, and gave her the registration numbers.

'So we've one more day to spend,' began Love, and then the telephone rang. I was nearest, so I picked it up.

'Personal call for Monsieur le Directeur, Aristo Autos,' said the girl grandly.

'That's me.'

'From London.'

I heard George's voice.

'Hullo, hullo,' he said. 'I've seen Jacko. He says you owe him some needle and pin – gin - for what he knows about Black. He was a Joe. Joe Rook. Crook. Used to drive getaway cars. Very good at it, too. But not quite good enough last time. He was serving ten years, but got out on some legal technicality. Misdirection of the jury. Some crap like that.'

'That won't help him now. Like I said, he's dead.'

'It happens to the nicest people,' said George. 'How?'

'I told you. A bullet.'

'Who fired it?'

'Someone hunting boar.'

'Oh, yes. You did tell me. Well, that's a new one on me – boar – whore,' chuckled George. 'You don't want to hunt it, mate. You want to wait until it comes roaring after you, steaming, rich and hot.'

'Thanks for the advice,' I said. 'But how we're all placed here now, it doesn't apply. I'm expecting to be back within days. We're packing up. Tell you all when I see you.'

I replaced the receiver.

'Who was that?' asked Amsterdam.

'My mechanic,' I said. 'Says this fellow ex-director of yours, Black, had a record.'

'Why should he ring now and tell you?'

'A mutual friend had just told him. He thought I might be interested.'

'Hm. Well, gentlemen, the insurance people are due any minute. Meanwhile, I'll settle the bills. If you order anything to eat or drink later on, you'll have to pay cash. And be ready to move at five o'clock tomorrow evening.'

We went down the stairs to the bar. A couple of men were sitting there in dark suits, and polished plastic shoes. Despite the sun, their faces were pale as though they lived under flat stones; their hair was black and spiky, dusted with grey. They could only be undertaker's assistants, insurance agents, or plain-clothes men. They were plain clothes men. One flashed a plastic identity card at me, which was better than flashing the other thing in a crowded place.

'Could we ask you a few questions, monsieur? he asked politely enough but with the policeman's underlying hardness to his voice. He intended to ask them whatever we said.

'What about?'

'The fire at the chateau. I believe you were with the Vicomte when it happened?'

'You believe correctly.'

'Tell me in your own words what happened.'

'I can't use anyone else's,' I said. 'I was in the car breaker's yard some miles up the road. A local, Charles Bonheur, came up and said he knew of two old cars that might interest me. He took me to the chateau, and introduced me to the Vicomte. We were alone in the house which seemed to be shuttered and locked, and I saw that the Vicomte was blind.

'I went upstairs to look around the place. He followed me up - and suddenly there was an explosion and he was caught in the flames. I was lucky to get out through a chimney.'

I looked them straight in the eyes as I spoke, because there's a myth that people never tell lies when they are looking right at you. Like most myths, it's not wholly true. The best liars look the most honest men. That's why they are the best liars.

'You may know, monsieur, that the Vicomte had a great collection of last war arms and ammunition, and some later items, too?'

'So he told me.'

'It is possible that some of these arms exploded and so hindered the work of the fire brigade?'

'I suppose so,' I said. After all, anything was possible if you were gullible enough to believe it. People once used to think the earth was flat-and that all car dealers were honest.

The policeman opened a cigar packet and offered me one; it was his way of telling me I was in no trouble.

'And, also, although it was a long time ago now, the Vicomte collaborated willingly with the Nazis,' he went on. 'He was blinded in an ambush by the Maquis. They were actually after someone else, but he would never believe this. He never forgave the people round here. And some of them, I know, never forgave him.

'There is a proverb, Nothing is longer than a Corsican's memory, monsieur. So he developed, shall we say, certain complexes. He felt, for instance, that his estates were being constantly encroached upon by people who remembered the wartime days. Those were hard times. Do you know that the Germans needed one hundred thousand troops here, to keep down two hundred thousand Corsicans - one soldier to every two civilians?'

Just for a second, fire smouldered in his shrouded eyes. The Greeks; the Romans; the Genoese; the British briefly in the late eighteenth century, and then the Germans even more briefly during the war, had all imposed their will on these islanders, and had withdrawn. The man shrugged; he had no need to say more. He lit both cigars and handed one to me.

'The Vicomte knew he was not liked or respected. He felt his rights were being eroded, and his privacy invaded.'

'It is all very sad,' I said, and it was. I'd ruined a good suit, nearly ruptured myself crawling up the chimney - and I hadn't even made a deal at the end of it. All I'd done was to save my life - and even this I really owed to Dr. Love.

Then I remembered the Bucciali and the Voisin. All was not yet irrevocably lost.

'Those two old cars of his I went to see. Who owns them now?'

'I believe there are cousins in Paris, but the local notaire, Monsieur Voltaire Rossi, dealt with his matters. He could inform you.'

'Thank you,' I said. 'Now, can I help you gentlemen in any other way? Any time you want a car, guaranteed used - and that's all that's guaranteed, remember - one owner, district nurse or late property of an Anglican bishop, only driven for ecclesiastical purposes, please apply to me.'

'It will be our pleasure. And if it is necessary, we could take a statement from you - a signed one?'

'Of course. But you'll have to come quickly, as the whore told the dawdler when she saw another client approaching. We leave tomorrow.'

'If one is needed, we will return today, monsieur.'

I waited until their car had driven away, then approached the receptionist. 'Where can I find Monsieur Rossi's office?' I asked him.

'In Corte, monsieur. Past the Foreign Legion barracks on the left, and you will see an alleyway. His is the fourth house down there. He has a brass plate.'

'Better than having a brass arse,' I said. But the man didn't understand the joke. These foreigners! Will it be different when we've been longer in the Common Market?

I borrowed Amsterdam's Simca again and drove into Corte, past the little red and white metal notices nailed to trees and contemptuously spattered with bullet holes: *Chasse Gardee.* Then, past the race track; on beyond piles of cork-bark waiting at the roadside to be collected, to the barracks, where shaven-headed Legionnaire sentries in well-pressed K.D., with white kepis and green epaulettes stood on guard, and into the former capital of Corsica.

I parked the car and there, just as the man said, in an alleyway so narrow that two bicycles could barely pass, with cobbles greasy from urine and slops, where doorsteps stuck out like broken fingernails over the narrow pavement, stood a house with a brass plate a couple of feet square, with the information 'Voltaire Rossi-Notaire,' stamped on it.

I walked into the hall paved with black and white tiles, like a huge chequer board. I knew how pawns must feel in a chess game; it was an apt floor for a lawyer's office. A Clapham junction of electric cables was pinned along the ceiling, and an ancient glass globe burned dimly, throbbing with the beat of some hidden asthmatic dynamo, although it was sunny outside.

Under a slow-turning fan, an old woman sat behind a desk, pecking like a parrot at an upright Olivetti. Her hair was drawn back in a big bun. She looked up, frowning at me in a short-sighted way.

'I wish to see Monsieur Rossi,' I told her.

'You have an appointment?' she asked as though even death could not come calling on Monsieur Rossi except by prior arrangement.

'Regrettably, no.'

'It is important?' she asked.

'A matter of life and death,' I said. 'Mostly the latter. About Monsieur le Vicomte at the chateau.'

She pushed back her chair, so that it scraped the tiles like a file, opened a door behind her and went into another room. Then she put her head around the door and said: 'He will see you now,'

Rossi's room was larger than I had expected, panelled in grey wood with a brass candelabra. Rossi was standing by the window, his back against white net curtains. He was an old, tall man, who had probably been old the day he was born. His face was the colour of lawyers' parchment, his hair grey dust sprayed on a wrinkled scalp. He wore a thin suit of clerical grey, even grey suede shoes. If it had been dusk I wouldn't even have seen him. He looked like a long moth with grey wings folded.

'You wish to see me, monsieur?' he asked in English.

I bowed.

'I appreciate your kindness in admitting me, without an appointment,' I said. 'I understand you act for Monsieur le Vicomte?'

He made a vague sign of the cross, which is better than some other signs I have seen.

'We *acted* for him, monsieur,' he admitted. 'He has, unfortunately, perished in a holocaust.'

A nice word, holocaust, I thought. Why couldn't the nutter say a fire? But then he was a lawyer; the longer words they use, the more money they can charge. Have you ever noticed how when they talk about money, they refer to it as *monies?* Always in the plural. Take the cash and let the credit go, as Omar Khayyam advised the dealer in used chariots.

I stood for a moment, wondering what Monsieur Rossi's cut

would be from the estate; whether he had already telephoned the property developers for their offers, or whether he had just bent the will in his direction: all is not grey that glitters.

'I know that, monsieur,' I told him. 'In fact, I was in the house near him when it happened.'

'Really?'

For a moment, the nearest thing to animation I had yet seen appeared in his face. Just a flicker of light in his eyes, faint as a drifting chip of ice on a foggy grey sea, but it showed he lived and breathed.

'Yes. I deal in cars of great vintage, which do not always have a money value, but shall we say, a value to those who love tradition,' I said cautiously. There was no point in pushing up the price before we started to haggle. Always let the other man be reinforced in his view that he is far cleverer than you; he generally is, anyway.

'I was taken to the Vicomte's chateau by someone who worked for him, one Charles Bonheur. He told me the Vicomte owned two French cars of some rarity, although not perhaps of great monetary value. I wondered whether the Vicomte would sell them.

'But since he is so regrettably dead, could you tell me who I should approach? After a decent interval, of course. One does not wish to intrude in private grief, does one?'

'One does not,' agreed the Notaire. 'But in this case it is common knowledge that, unfortunately, great as were the Vicomte's qualities as a man, as an aristocrat and as the last resident member of one of the most powerful and oldest families in Corsica, he has no one here to mourn him.'

'How very sad,' I said cheerfully. 'So who should I apply to?'

'I dealt with his affairs, and they are, of course, personal.'

'Of course.'

'However, it is no secret, and I am betraying no confidence, nor am I violating the sacred trust between lawyer and client, when I tell you that, while the chateau, the estate, and other properties have been left to relations in France, all his cars and the garden equipment have been left to the former employee you mention, Monsieur Charles Bonheur."

'So what you are telling me, Monsieur Notaire, is that I should see Monsieur Bonheur, and make him an offer?'

'In one word - yes.'

'In two words,' I said. 'Thank you.' We shook hands gravely, neither trusting the other, and I went out of the room leaving him standing there against the curtains, looking into a grey future, or possibly a rosy one.

Now I had two reasons for wanting to see Bonheur. The other reason was personal; to find why he had tried to shoot me on the roof. And I also had an uneasy feeling right down inside me that I would be wise to find him before he came looking for me. That way, I would be the hunter, not the hunted. And this, in Corsica, was the season of the chase.

CHAPTER SEVEN

I had a drink in a pavement cafe, then I decided to drive to the lake, the Etang, to see whether anything had been done about salvaging my boat - or finding Jean-Paul.

In the excitement of meeting Love, I had completely forgotten to ask him whether he had any news of the man, but I was inclined to think he hadn't or he would have told me. So I drove back to the dreary crossroads at Catareggio, past the shacks which in ten years' time would no doubt be replaced by skyscrapers and high-rise hotels, down the track through the trees to the lake.

An old Jeep with a crane on it had been backed down into the water, and two men in swimming trunks and flippers were rowing in a boat towards the centre of the lake, paying out their rope from the crane behind them. Amsterdam stood alone on the edge of the scummy water. , 'So you took my car,' he began accusingly.

I admitted it. I couldn't do anything else, for I was actually driving the thing.

'Next time,' he went on, 'do me a small favour. *Ask* me. I had to scrounge a lift with these buggers.' He inclined his head towards the two men in the boat.

'Insurance men?' I asked.

He nodded.

'Those bastards will have their pound of flesh. Better them than me. I've a bad heart. That water looks too cold for me.'

A few wasps buzzed around us; the fish went on leaping out of the water.

'Have a look through these,' said Amsterdam, handing me his binoculars.

I focused them. The rowing boat had reached the buoy and

they were tying up to it. Then one of the men moved to one side and the boat dipped under his weight. He wore a yellow oxygen cylinder strapped to his back. He adjusted his mask and went over backwards in the way of the trained skin-diver. The other man waited in the stern.

The boat bobbed slightly as the first man surfaced, pushing up his mask. He swung himself aboard. His companion waved to the shore, the Jeep driver started his engine, and the winch began to turn, gears screaming with rust. The Jeep shuddered and its tyres bit into the soft, glue-like mud as the rope tightened. The engine backfired once, and went on running.

Slowly, the taut rope lifted out of the water, throwing off spray like silver dust. A soft ripple wrinkled the smooth, glassy surface of the lake. Then bits of weed, half a branch of submerged tree, slimy and stuck with mussels, came out of the water, and after it the hull of my boat, white like bone.

The two men began to row in. They waded ashore, and as the bows came up, they shook the hull from side to side to throw out some of the water it had shipped. Then they turned it on its side, white and useless, like some huge dead shell from the lake bed. The seats and steering wheel were undamaged, but the windscreen had been torn away. A huge hole gaped like a shark's mouth in the fibreglass hull. The engine trailed fronds of weed; oil was still seeping out, mixing in rainbow colours with a pool of water on the shore.

'Well, there she is,' Amsterdam told everyone dramatically. 'There's your actual boat. You can check the engine number. That proves she went down.'

'We never doubted *that,* monsieur,' said one of the men. He saw me standing there and our eyes met, locked, and passed. He was the plain-clothes policeman who had spoken to me in the hotel.

'They are police,' I told Amsterdam, in case he still thought they were simply insurance narks.

'I don't care a bugger who they are,' he said indifferently, and turned away and began to walk towards his car. I followed him and only looked back once. That was enough. The two men stood, watching us.

We drove back to the Caselle in silence.

'Come and have a drink,' said Amsterdam as we turned into the drive. 'I hate drinking on my own.'

I went to his room with him. Clothes were thrown over his bed, with shirts and ties and lightweight jackets. It looked like a men's changing room, not one person's bedroom. He must be packing to go. I noticed, for the first time, the little glass bottles of pills. Maybe he did have a bad heart. Well, his experiences here couldn't be doing it any. good.

'How much has all this cost you?' I asked.

'Me, personally, nothing,' he said. 'The first rule of being a success in this business, or any other, is never spend your own money.'

'A fair philosophy,' I said.

'You have to be a philosopher in films,' he replied, 'or you'd shoot your bloody self. Only one thing bothers me - whether I should quit now, as I told you and Dr. Love - or change my mind and stay on and try the sequence again. But elsewhere in Corsica.'

'You haven't a crew,' I reminded him. 'And we're booked on the ferry.'

'Those aren't problems. We can hire a French camera team easily enough, and cancel our bookings.'

'Let me know what you decide,' I said. We had a pastis each, but his mind was obviously on other things, so I went over to the bar on my own. I had thought my way of earning a living was crazy until I heard his. But then, one half of the world has literally no idea how the other half lives, and they never believe it when they're told.

For example, whenever I attend a car auction, I usually slip a fiver to the porter to tell me whether any other interested bidders are around.

Once, a porter I knew whispered that someone else had just slipped him the same amount to discover who was the sharpest buyer.

I was bidding that day for two Red Label Bentleys, so called simply because they happened to have a red backing to the 'B' on their radiator badges. Others had green or black or blue backgrounds, usually to tone with the original colour scheme of the car. But now they've become a status symbol: a Black Label, a Green Label and so on, which really means as much or as little as the colour of a label on a sauce bottle. Such is the power of snobbery.

As I approached my ceiling price for these cars - one which, of course, would still give me a clear hundred per cent profit after all expenses - I saw that this other buyer would deliberately edge past me by fifty or a hundred quid. I let him, for he was obviously rich, and I just wanted to become rich. Finally, he bought the cars for about two hundred more than I was prepared to pay, so I let them go and forgot about the incident.

I remembered it a month later when I received a letter from some old woman who explained that a relation had recently passed away - it is odd how people rarely admit in writing that anyone has *died.* They have always passed away, or are called to higher service, or go beyond the veil - when, in fact, they are dead as a bounced cheque, and the undertakers are already picking the gold fillings out of their teeth and preparing to switch their expensive coffins for something cheaper before they slide them past the Bunsens in the crematorium.

Anyhow, this dear and departed relation had left two old Bentley Red Label cars to her. She wondered whether I would be interested in buying them.

I went along to see the cars, which were the same Red Labels for which the unknown buyer had outbid me.

I asked Jacko Jackson to find out what was behind this little arrangement, which was too contrived to be genuine, as the man told the girl who wore three falsies instead of two. He discovered that the buyer at the auction was an arms dealer who sold ex-

Army surplus to revolutionaries and any other would-be assassins willing to pay in notes for the means of supplying sudden death to others. He'd pick up £10,000 in notes on a deal, but so much money was too warm to keep under his bed, and banks didn't like to accept it in case income tax inspectors asked questions.

So after each deal, he went to silver sales and vintage car auctions, found out which professional buyers he should watch and then carefully outbid them. A few weeks later, he would offer the silver to fine art dealers and the old cars to people like me. So he wisely and cautiously cooled money that would otherwise be too hot to handle.

We live and learn, but some of us don't live long enough, and others never learn quickly enough. And some, like Black, die before they learn the first and basic lesson of life: which is, keep your long nose out of other people's business, unless you want it shortened, and maybe your life with it. Which philosophical thought brought me back to my present situation.

I thought, for no reason at all, of words chalked on the wall, at one end of my mews: 'Jesus Saves'. Someone else had prudently added underneath, 'But Moses invests'. And that's what I should be doing - investing more thought to untangling this rats' nest of misfortunes.

Assuming first that a plane had come down in the lake, or that it had been brought down; then assuming that someone somewhere either knew who or what it contained or was determined to find out, had the pilot died in the crash - or was he alive, possibly in this village, maybe even in the Caselle? And if any, or all, or even none of these assumptions were true, what was there in it for me?

Because, if there was no cut, no slice, simply the cube root of F.A., then I was being a fool if I .became even more involved. Then I remembered the Voison and the Bucciali, and I knew I had to stay involved until I could lever those two beauties my way, as the fellow with the walking stick told the girl with the 42-inch knockers.

I had another drink, and I reached some conclusions, and went back to see Amsterdam.

'Have dinner with me,' I suggested.

'I'd love to, but I can't tonight. I've just had the insurance people on the phone again, and they say there are still some bits missing from the engine, and what am I going to do about it, then? If these bits and pieces hurt some bather or damaged another boat, they'd be liable. Ridiculous, in my view. But it's their view that carries weight.'

'So what are you going to do about it then?'

'I am thinking of going down myself after them.'

'I didn't know you were a diver.'

'The way they go on about these things, you'd think it was the most important thing in the world to bring up every screw, every bolt, every bit of rope. So I'll do my best. And then, if they still complain, sod them.'

'When are you going to dive?'

'It's calmest in the evening. Which is why I won't be able to join you. I can't eat before I dive, and afterwards, I'll probably be so shagged that all I'll be fit for is bed. On my own, of course.'

'Of course,' I said. 'But what about your bad heart? And the cold water?'

'I've got enough pills for the first, and I'll wear a wet suit against the second.'

I felt a bit sorry for him; he appeared dejected; maybe being a film producer wasn't so much fun after all. Maybe he really *was* a film producer? I went in search of Love, the doctor, not the other thing, but he was not in his room, and the receptionist said he thought that he and Victoria had gone into Venaco. So I had a drink on my own and then climbed into the London-Edinburgh and drove back along the empty roads to Catareggio, and then on to the lake. I wanted to see what Amsterdam dredged up from the sea-bed. I only passed one vehicle the whole way, a shabby Fiat van that pulled out from a cafe near the crossroads and overtook me as I turned off the main road.

This time I did not go right down to the beach, but turned the car off the track into the bushes and parked it concealed by branches, facing the road. I sat at the wheel for a few moments after I had switched off the almost silent engine. I could hear nothing but the crickets and the frogs, and in the distance, from some cafe in town, a sound of faint music. Then I climbed out, closed the door as gently as possible and walked down the track to the edge of the lake. My feet made no sound on the sand.

Amsterdam's Simca was already there, turned, like mine, towards the road. Presumably in case - like me - he had to make a quick getaway. But who or what would chase us? Obviously, we both feared someone. Did we fear the same person-and for the same reason?

It was already dusk, and mist rolled in over the silvery water, shrouding bushes and merging outlines, shrinking distance. The fish were still jumping. I stood, looking out into the gloom, hearing them leap and fall back, and the lap of the tiny waves at my feet. I could just see a bobbing black head at the limit of my vision. This would probably be Amsterdam.

I wondered if he'd started his dive, or whether he was finishing it; and then I saw a second head bob next to his, about six feet away to the left. Or was *this* Amsterdam? It was impossible to say in the deepening darkness.

I screwed up my eyes, straining them, but still could not make out anything more than these two bobbing black dots. Better them than me, I thought. It would be bitterly cold out there, even in a wet suit. I don't know what I had expected, but it was not this. Very likely, Amsterdam had asked one of the policemen or insurance men to dive with him, so they could see how anxious he was to help them. I felt vaguely and quite unreasonably disappointed, and turned to walk back to the car.

As I turned, I heard the faint snap of a small twig. The noise was too loud for an animal, and in any case, wild animals are timid and quiet and light on their feet after dark. Someone rather than something was in the bushes.

Was it only one of the raincoat brigade, who had seen the car parked and hoped to see something more exciting on the beach, or could this be someone on more sinister business? Maybe someone interested in the divers — or what they were diving for?

I bent down, felt around at my feet, picked up the largest stone I could find, and threw it back into the trees. It crashed through some branches and' thudded on the ground. Afterwards, there was no noise, no movement, no breathing. Perhaps I was being over-sensitive, over-cautious. What I had heard was probably only a dead branch breaking; the sort of thing that happened a hundred times a day and you thought nothing of it, simply because it was day. Night adds fear to the simplest sound.

I turned towards the car, and as I turned the whole damp evening, the gloomy bushes, the path I could now scarcely see, exploded in blinding splinters of light.

Pain drove a sharpened spike through my head. And then there was nothing but darkness so deep that I could not even see a falling star. And I was falling faster than any star.

I was lying on the beach and my body was bent like a broken axle spring.

The moon was moving up the sky now, shining through the mist like a gas lamp through a gauze curtain. My head seemed to have been hammered into my body, and the backs of my eyes had been sandpapered in my skull. Every joint ached, and I was rigid with cold, my muscles locked tight as though the joints had been bolted in position.

I stood up very shakily. I had a lump on my head the size of a plover's egg, and plovers lay big eggs. Whoever had hit me, had hit me hard. I'd do the same for him if I found out who he was. No, not if. *When* I found him.

I began to shuffle slowly along the path towards the car. I glanced back once at the water. There was no sign of any bobbing heads; no sign, either, of Amsterdam's car. I was on my own.

I approached the Rolls cautiously, but no one seemed to

be near it. The moon shone silver on its radiator and dash-board; I climbed in behind the wheel and switched on the ignition. As the engine fired, I drove out as quickly as I could. The town was deserted; one street lamp burned from a wire stretched above the crossroads; a stray cat turned terrified green eyes on me and melted into the shadows. I melted away just as silently towards the Caselle.

I parked the car, and walked slowly and painfully to my chalet. The bed was turned down. I sat on it, feeling the lump on my head. Then I found my Essolube bottle and swallowed some whisky. It swam through my aching body and cheered me. At least I wasn't dead. Where there was life there was hope. The clichés began to return, and with them some feeling to my joints.

I washed my face in cold water in the basin and glanced at my watch. A quarter to one. It must be Tuesday. If it wasn't, I couldn't still be in Corsica, for we were leaving that night.

I went out of my chalet, swayed along the path between the herbs and bushes, and knocked on Love's door. I heard a grunt and went in and switched on the light.

Love sat up in bed, blinking.

'What the hell's the matter?'

'I've been hit on the head,' I told him.

'Then you'd better come to the surgery tomorrow. I'm not seeing patients now.'

'I'm not a patient. I'm a friend.'

I sat down shakily on the edge of his bed, and he felt the lump.

'A bit more to the right, and you'd have been dead,' he said. 'As it is, you will have a headache for a couple of hours, but you'll live. And that will cost you ten guineas. Old money.'

'I'll pay it in kind,' I said. 'Old kind. Cord spares.'

Then I told him what had happened, and where.

'You didn't get a glimpse of who hit you?'

'Nothing,' I said. 'But there were two men - two swimmers at least - in the lake. I saw their heads bobbing around.'

Love swung himself out of bed.

'Let's see where the others are.'

He pulled on a dressing gown, opened the cupboard and took out a black, square-edged suitcase. He opened it on the bed.

'My travelling surgery,' he said proudly. 'Almost everything here that I have at home. Even a cylinder of nitrous oxide if I need to put you to sleep!'

'I'll have a pill instead, doctor,' I told him.

He unscrewed the lid from a plastic jar and shook out two yellow capsules.

'Take these,' he said. 'They'll see you live the night.'

I swallowed them, and felt neither better nor worse. Then, seconds later, it was as though a bomb was exploding inside me, slowly with feeling. I was suddenly taut, and like Sir Lancelot, whose strength was as the strength often; not in my case, because my heart was pure, but because the pills were so damned strong.

We went out to Amsterdam's room and my feet only touched the ground a couple of times. Adrenalin surged round my body like 105 octane petrol. I would live for ever.

Love knocked. No answer. He opened the door, and switched on the light. The room was empty. Bedclothes were rumpled on the floor. Drawers had been torn open. A cupboard door swung out on its hinges. Even the carpet had been ripped up. Across the bed lay a frogman's suit, still wet, but without a frogman inside it; not even Amsterdam, who was as near a frog as any man I knew.

'Where is he?' asked Love.

His bags had disappeared with him, but he had left a silk tie over the back of a chair, and a clean shirt with his initials on the pocket, so he must have left hurriedly, without time to pack properly.

There had either been a struggle, or someone had come in looking for Amsterdam - or something he believed Amsterdam had hidden - after Amsterdam had gone. And where was he now?

'Let's see Victoria,' said Love. 'She may have heard something.'

We switched off the light and went out again to Victoria's chalet. Again, no answer. We went inside, switched on her light. The room was neat and empty.

I crossed over to the dressing table. A letter was pushed under a glass ashtray. It was addressed to me, so I opened it. (I only put this in to make me sound an O.K. person; actually, I'd have opened it whoever it was addressed to.)

'I have had to leave unexpectedly,' I read. 'Will wait for you in Ajaccio. This is a personal thing, so give any explanation you like to the others. Will see you at the ferry with the Alpine around nine tomorrow evening. Victoria.'

'I didn't hear a car leave,' said Love.

'That Rolls doesn't make a lot of noise, even if it is fifty years old.'

'Even so . . .'

Love sat down on the edge of the bed and lit a Gitane, and blew a smoke ring reflectively.

'What strikes you as being the strangest thing about this whole trip?' he suddenly asked me.

'The fact I haven't had a piece of tail since I've been here, not even a touch. And to me that's so strange on any foreign trip, it's almost worth writing to *The Times* about.'

'As a medical man, I could advise you that abstinence is not necessarily deleterious to your health.'

'I'm not thinking of my health,' I retorted.

'But apart from what to you appears to be a basic anachronism of all foreign travel, we are supposed to be here to make a film. Yet we've still not seen a camera, an actor or any crew. Now we're even lacking a producer — and our girl driver. One man's been killed. You've been nearly burned alive, and now knocked out. Where is all this getting us?'

I couldn't say, and suddenly I didn't greatly care; I had had enough. The effects of the pills were beginning to weaken. I could feel a very small hammer begin to beat inside my head as though a woodpecker was trying in a half-hearted way to tap his way out. Maybe I would not live for ever after all.

'I am going to bed,' I told Love. 'I'll tell you my theory in the morning.'

We walked back through the chilly darkness together. I went into my chalet, locked my door, pulled off my clothes. I had a quick bath and climbed thankfully into bed. The day thou gavest, Lord, had finally ended. And I wasn't at all .sorry that it had.

CHAPTER EIGHT

I must have fallen asleep, for the next thing I recall was lying there, listening, my eyes open, my brain running slowly like the flywheel in a bull-nose Morris Cowley.

I could make out a square of curtain lighter against the window, and shapes of furniture in the room; this meant the time could be around two o'clock. A dog was howling miles away; the only other sound was the solid roar from the river. But neither of these noises had woken me up. I lay still, holding my breath (which is sometimes wiser than holding the other thing). Then I heard the faint sigh of someone else breathing, and the creak of a dry board under a rug, the tiny scrape of a chair leg. Someone was in the room with me. I rolled over on one side in case I had to move quickly.

'Stay exactly where you are,' I said, 'or I'll blow your nuts off.'

This was boasting, of course, for the only weapon I had was the one with which nature had armed me, but it gave me a second to roll right across the bed and .switch on the light.

Victoria was standing in the room, her back to the window. She must have climbed in over the verandah.

'Amendment,' I said. 'For nuts, read knockers.'

'Is that a threat or a promise?'

'Neither. Fact,' I told her. 'What the hell are you doing here? You should be in Ajaccio by now.'

'You have been in my room then?'

'Yes.'

'I changed my mind about going.'

'Why?'

'I'm afraid,' she said simply, and sat down on the edge of the bed.

'What of? Me?' I was being hopeful.

She shook her head, smiling. I thought of adding: 'You would be, if you knew what I had in the bed with me,' but this seemed neither the right time nor place.

I moved over to give her some room.

'I've been asleep,' I said, which was pretty obvious. 'I do my best thinking in a lying position.'

'Is that all you do best in that position?' she said.

'Try me,' I suggested.

She put out her hand to switch off the light. I heard the rustle as her clothes came off. Then she was under the sheets, her body, long and warm and soft against mine. Although I know that good tunes are sometimes played on old riddles, they are usually only tunes, not great music. You can't beat young meat, as the cat-food man said.

'Can you think of a better way to spend an evening?' I asked her.

'I'll give you my opinion later,' she replied, and from then on we found ourselves without much time for conversation. What with one thing and another - but mostly with one thing - time wore running shoes, and it must have been nearly five o'clock before I finally reached out and put on the light and sat up in that superior male way, while Victoria snuggled down in the sheets, her black hair spread like a fan against her whiteness.

I thought for a mad moment of having a quick short back and sides, one for the road, sort of thing, but decided against it. After all, there's a time for toil and a time for tail. Now, it was question-time. Why was she frightened — and why had she really come into my room? Not just for what had happened, although that might be a part of it.

I rolled her over.

'No, not again,' she protested. 'I'm asleep.'

'You're not. And you are going to talk. *Why* are you afraid?'

She opened her eyes then, and I could see myself mirrored in those green touch-paper pupils, so recently lit.

Then suddenly, and against all expectation - which shows you can spend a lifetime trying to learn about women and end up, like me, knowing nothing - Victoria began to cry.

'What's the matter?' I asked her.

'You wouldn't understand,' she said.

'I could learn to.'

'I was thinking about my husband,' she said.

'Why him, especially?' Maybe she was worried in case he suspected how she spent her evenings and was only looking for evidence to be rid of all her bills? And I hadn't even guessed she was married!

'Because I'll never see him again,' she said.

'You didn't appear to be worrying much about that just now.'

'You *don't* understand,' she repeated. 'He's dead.'

'Who was he?' I asked, not really caring; in fact, rather relieved. After all, if he were dead, he couldn't put the button on me.

'He was Black,' she said. 'Robert Black.'

Now it was my turn to roll over in the bed rather smartly.

'Did you come out here with him?' I asked her.

'No.'

'But it's hardly a coincidence you are - were - here together?'

She snuggled against me. I didn't object, even though I knew from experience that such sudden warmth in some women often precedes a load of lies.'

'I divorced him two years ago.'

'So?'

'So when he was behind with the alimony - which was nearly all the time - if he heard of any jobs going - walk-on parts, crowd scenes, the odd TV commercial - he passed them on to.me. Saved him paying anything.'

'He knew Amsterdam well?'

'Yes. Yes, he did.'

She seemed as though she was going to say some more, and then thought better of it.

'Tell me more about him,' I said, and lay back, looking up at the ceiling, wondering how many other men had lain like this in this same bed with other women and asked them about their husbands. And how many of them had told these women that their wives didn't understand them, when the trouble was that they all understood each other far too well; they were like books they had read too often.

'I divorced him because he was always in and out of jail.'

'That's habit forming,' I told her, thinking of another habit I could form very easily with her. 'What was he in for last?'

'Getaway driver,' she said, confirming what George had told me. 'Jewel robbery. He drove very well, very fast. He specialised in jewel jobs. Knew a lot about gems. Before he started driving, he did a bit of smuggling.'

'By car?' My mind flickered back over all kinds of people I had known who had smuggled the widest variety of items from watches to jewels to drugs in spare tyres, dummy petrol tanks, battery cases, arm-rests, roof-linings, tins of oil, windscreen washer tanks; some very successfully, and some only once.

'No,' said Victoria. 'Plane.'

The word instantly alerted my memory bank, such as it was. I remembered the Vicomte telling me in the chateau about the plane he had brought down. Black could have been the pilot. But then so could any other of the 3,478,000 odd registered private pilots about the world.

I wasn't any nearer to anything important, so I asked: 'How did he become involved here with Amsterdam?'

'I don't know,' she said. 'But several times Amsterdam had been the go-between in odd deals. The runner. The man who raises money, who runs from place to place until the whole thing is stitched together.'

'Has he a record, too?'

'Of course,' she said, surprised at the question. 'In his world you're on a pretty narrow ledge. Fall on one side, you get knighted for political and public services. Fall on the other, you go down for five years.'

'Then I think I'll stay lying on my back, as I am,' I said, and drew her on top of me.

Afterwards, when I lay looking at the ceiling, I said suddenly, as though the thought had just struck me with all the force of the Queen's Proctor laying a hand on a guilty husband: 'You said your husband smuggled things by plane?'

'Yes.'

'You know a plane came down in that lake at Catareggio a week or so ago?'

She stiffened against me, which minutes before would have done all sorts of things to me, but not now. I was like the old roué who said that when he was young, he had four supple members and one stiff, but now he was old he had four stiff members and one supple.

'Who told you?'

'A man I met here.'

'Do you think Amsterdam knows?'

'Is that important?' I asked.

I remembered the two swimmers under the moon, the rustle in the bushes from someone else who was watching them, and watching me. I remembered the blow on my head. Whether Amsterdam knew or not, someone else knew, and someone wanted that plane out of the water, or at least whatever it had contained. Diamonds could have been as valuable a cargo as any other.

'Did your husband fly that plane?' I asked.

'I didn't know there *was* a plane,' she said simply. 'I only knew it was desperately important for him to be here. He promised me five thousand pounds against all my alimony if I came here, too.'

'So you fixed that with Amsterdam?'

'Yes.'

'Who do you think shot your ex-husband?'

'How could I possibly know? It was an accident.'

'A very strange accident. One man with one shot hits someone in the forehead in a speedboat. If there'd been a lot of wild shooting after boars, or whatever else around the lake, bullets whanging around like fireworks, I could understand it. But there wasn't. There was only one man, one marksman, with his rifle. The murderer.'

And had this unknown marksman, for some reason I did not know, meant to shoot me instead of Black? Perhaps he had aimed at me as a warning to Black - and perhaps he had hit the wrong man. Suddenly, I wanted to be away from these uneasy thoughts. I climbed out of bed and dressed quickly.

'Where are you going?' Victoria asked in surprise.

I had no idea, so I just said, 'Out.'

'Are you coming back?'

'Unless I'm shot on the way.'

And if anyone was waiting for me outside, either in the bushes or across the river, this might not be so absurd as it sounded. Bonheur. He was the only man I'd seen with a gun. Now where the hell was he? And Jean-Paul? So much had happened so quickly that I'd still forgotten to ask Love about him. I would do so now.

I looked at my watch; half past seven. I walked over to the main hotel building. A waiter was flicking a cloth over tabletops. I wished him *'Bonjour'*, which cost me nothing, and I hoped he'd had as good a night as I had.

I then ordered black coffee, croissants and honey, and two lightly boiled eggs, which reminded me of that old gag about the young girl who dreamed she was a lightly boiled egg and woke up to find somebody going to work on her.

Love came in, looking fresh, as though he had been carefully laundered. He had obviously spent a more restful night than me. While the waiter shuffled about, we made talk so minuscule it wasn't even small. Then, when we were alone, I asked him about Jean-Paul.

'There was no sign of him around the lake,' he said. 'I searched everywhere. And I asked Amsterdam, who seemed equally mystified. He's just disappeared.'

'I'll be glad when I can do the same thing,' I told him. 'The vibes in this place are all wrong. Someone's out to get me and I don't know who or why.'

I didn't, either. It wasn't even as though I'd sold anyone a car.

Love pushed a piece of paper across the table at me. It wasn't a bill, so I picked it up. It was dated the previous day. I read: 'Dr. Love. In your absence, the British Consul rang. Could you kindly present yourself at his office, with your friend, at 10.30 tomorrow morning? You are both required to sign a document regarding the shooting accident.'

'I'm doing nothing else,' I said. 'Or no one. Let's drive over together.'

At least I would be away from the hotel, and a moving target was always more difficult to hit. If I kept moving until we sailed from Ajaccio that evening, I should be safe. Or so I told myself.

We finished breakfast and I walked out to the garage.

'Here's the Alpine back,' said Love.

'Yes. Victoria didn't go to Ajaccio after all. She's back, too.'

'Is she now?'

He looked at me and smiled; I smiled at him.

'Let's take that car, then,' he said.

'She's got the key,' I said. 'I don't want to wake her up.'

'Your delicacy does you credit,' he said, and opened the door of the Cord.

The consulate had been open for half an hour by the time we reached it. A couple of English web-foots were sitting in the waiting room wearing unattractive English clothes; shorts too long, shirts the wrong colour, pale, sweaty pustuled flesh showing through open collars. I guessed they'd lost their passports and were here to beg money for the return fare. And I thought of the elegant consular officials endeavouring to conceal their distaste at these shabby, shoddy representatives of the island race. I didn't bother to conceal my own - as the defendant in the raincoat told the magistrate on another occasion.

'Can I help you?' the girl behind the enquiries desk asked me brightly.

I thought she could, but not in the way she meant. Dr. Love

threw me a glance in lieu of anything else to keep me quiet, and said, 'Yes. I am Dr. Love. I believe you wish me to sign some papers in connection with that boat accident in the Etang the other day?'

'I don't think so, doctor,' she said. 'Not to my knowledge, anyway.'

'But we had a message from the consul last night. He asked us to come here at half past ten this morning.'

'The consul wasn't here last night. He was in Ajaccio, on business. He is not here this morning, either. These two gentlemen are waiting to see him.'

'Bloody right we are,' said one of them, pushing back his flat cap. 'I've been waiting here half an hour. Don't know what I pay rates for.'

'You don't pay rates,' I said, guessing. 'You live in a council flat.'

'Oo're you?' he asked belligerently.

'P. Rick's my name, Prick,' I said. 'A close relation of yours.'

'Really!' exclaimed the girl looking from one to the other of us in horror.

'Don't mind him,' said Dr. Love soothingly. 'He's receiving treatment.'

'So I should think,' said the girl. 'I wonder what foreigners think we are like at home!'

'Never mind what they think we are like at home,' I said. 'What about this message?'

I hate all this ponce-hogging around. Let's get on with the deal. Time spent in talk is nearly always wasted.

'I know absolutely nothing about that. I was on duty here last night and I certainly didn't send any message to Dr. Love.'

She opened a drawer in the desk and took out a file and fanned through the pages.

'Here are all the documents on the accident. There's nothing further we need to bother you with, doctor.'

'Thank you,' said Love. 'There must have been a mistake.'

We went out into the street and stood for a moment on the

steps.

'Do you think there *was* a call?' I asked.

'The receptionist gave me the note, which is not proof, of course. But why should anyone go to the trouble of writing down the message if there wasn't one? Unless...'

'Unless someone wanted us out of the way today.'

'Yes. But who?'

'Let's have a drink first,' I said. 'Or several. Lubricate the brain cells.'

The cafe didn't seem to sell anything other than pastis, so we drank a couple each and then drove back. There was more traffic on the roads now, mostly tourists in hired cars, weaving about or parking on blind corners taking photographs, pointing out the spot where Napoleon had stopped to pee, or whatever other interesting historical event had happened there.

Outside the Caselle, a white coach with German number plates was vomiting its cargo of American tourists on to the park: women with blue hair wrapped in plastic covers, beat-up, dried-out old men in Dacron suits, skins withered and faces wrinkled as tortoise necks, a long way from Des Moines and Little Rock and worried whether the water was safe to drink.

The receptionist was out greeting them and he waved two envelopes at us.

'The bill is already paid,' he announced. 'Monsieur Amsterdam and Mademoiselle Bassett have left these notes for you.'

So they had both gone. The man handed over two envelopes. I gave one to Love and opened the other. A few lines were scribbled in pencil on a piece of hotel stationery: 'What you told me last night about the plane frightened me. Amsterdam has decided to find some new location, but I have told him I must leave after all. He quite agrees. I am taking the Rolls to Ajaccio and will put it on the ferry. I will leave it at your garage in Belgravia. V.'

'What did Amsterdam say?' I asked Love. We exchanged letters.

'I tried to contact you, but was told you were out. I have heard of a better location, near Porto. So I will look at it before pulling out completely as I intended. I have paid all the bills, and will see you in the Hotel de la Tour, Porto. There we can either go on to Ajaccio or stay there.'

So what would happen if he decided to stay? We could cancel our ferry bookings easily enough, but the only way of reaching Victoria would be to drive all the way to Ajaccio and bring back her car. So presumably she had left before Amsterdam heard of the new location - or she simply hadn't told him she was going so quickly. Either way, there was nothing in it for me, as the undertaker told the fellow who rose from the dead.

'Did you see them go?' Love asked the receptionist.

'No, sir. I have been very busy. This package tour has just arrived unexpectedly.'

'Another thing,' said Love. 'That call from the British Consul. They know nothing about it. Who took the message here last night?'

'I did, monsieur. I wrote it down for you.'

'I see,' said Love, not seeing any more than me; or if he did, not liking what he saw.

'Now, monsieur,' said the receptionist. 'If you will excuse me.'

We excused him and walked out to the swimming pool. The sun was warm, and the water splashed and glittered as some children kept jumping about in the shallow end; everything seemed very peaceful. We sat down under an umbrella.

'What time shall we leave?' I asked Love. I was in no hurry; nor was he.

'We'll have lunch, doze in the sun here this afternoon, then pack our gear, have a quick snack and set off,' he said.

'Won't Amsterdam be going out of his mind?'

'If he's a mind to leave, he may consider leaving it,' agreed Love. 'But if our experience here is any criterion, we will just be hanging about in Porto, too.

'Let us now adjourn to the restaurant. I intend to have a light lunch of mussels, then a hot lobster, split down the centre, cooked with saffron, and a bottle of the wine of the house.'

'I can think of only one thing I'd rather do,' I said.

'I believe the words of Confucius about food,' replied Love gravely.' "It is difficult to discover any other pleasure a man can enjoy three times a day, every day of his life, without tiring".'

'I'm looking for one, doctor,' I told him.

'I'm looking, too,' agreed Love, 'but not for that. For some reasonable explanation for our present situation. Why should Amsterdam go to all the trouble of hiring three cars, engaging us to bring them out here, to make a film and yet have no crew to film it? Now he's apparently going to repeat the performance elsewhere. Talk about a host of extras, there's not even *one* here — or there. Nowt's so strange as folk, but this is ridiculous.'

'We've been paid, at least.'

'Agreed, but not for doing what we were hired to do. As a doctor, if I treated a private patient for pneumonia, I would be surprised if I received a cheque from him in payment for treating a broken leg.'

'That's a gentleman's surprise, doctor. I'm only surprised when I *don't* get a cheque. Or when I do and it jumps like a frog on the deck, and the bank manager gets me by the throat when I try to cash it.'

'Maybe there are others who will get us by the throat before we're through,' said Love cheerfully. 'Unless, of course, we seize them first.'

On that philosophic note, we ordered lunch. I dozed most of the afternoon, and it was early evening, with a hint of chill in the air, like a mother-in-law's welcome, when I awoke. The pool looked a lot less attractive with shadows darkening the hills across the river. Love was standing by my side smoking one of his horrible French cigarettes. I stood up. It must be time for us to move.

'It's six o'clock,' said Love. 'We'll pack, have a light dinner and then - en *voiture.*'

'How are we for petrol?'

I still was only half awake.

'I have taken both cars out to Venaco and filled them up, while you were asleep.'

'If you want a job when you're struck off the roll, I'll let you have a reference.'

'I'd rather have money,' said Love.

He went into the bar while I walked back to my chalet, threw my few possessions into my bag, took a last glim around the room to make sure I'd left nothing behind, and then joined him for dinner.

Both our cars stood outside - my Rolls and his Cord — splendid anachronisms of the English twenties, the American thirties. Half a dozen people from the package tour stood around them admiringly, telling each other, with perfect truth, that they don't make them like that any more.

Never again will the world see six of every model Rolls make bought by standing order from one man — as happened with the Maharajah of Mysore in the nineteen-twenties. And can you imagine any buyer today specifying that the seats of his new car must be upholstered with the hides from *still-born* calves so that they will be completely free of blemishes? This was not an infrequent instruction by British aristos in the same decade. No, they don't make them like that any more - people and cars - and they never will again.

'I'll lead,' I told Love, when we had dumped our bags in his Cord, because it had a boot that locked.

I climbed in behind the wheel of the Rolls and started the big engine. It hummed for a moment, and then settled down, to its almost silent woofle, as though a giant were breathing deeply and peacefully beneath the bonnet. There was no mechanical noise - not because hundredweights of felt had been packed around the engine to muffle it, as big cars are cosseted today, but simply because of the craftsmanship of the men who had built it, when the factory insisted on so many tests, on bench, on rollers, then on the road, that the wonder was that the car wasn't worn out before it left the factory.

I pushed the gear lever through its gate, about as difficult as cutting warm butter with a sharpened knife, let out the clutch, and we were off. I often think that a modern, mass-produced car is like an extra armoured skin for the driver, which is why so many people drive so badly. They know that this metal shell will protect them from their boorish behaviour. It scuttles along like a tin beetle as close to the ground as its driver's thoughts, while, in an old open car, you command a view all other motorists miss.

You are above them physically and mentally, part Toad of Toad Hall, part Jonah Mansel of Dornford Yates' novels, swinging his Rolls through a world that acknowledged the inherent superiority of the pound sterling, and the Englishman who had it (the pound I mean) in his pocket.

The sun slid quickly down to the place where it slept behind the mountains, and the air was suddenly cool and heavy with scent from mint and myrtle and maquis. Then the sun disappeared altogether, and we drove through the brief Corsican dusk, tinged with blue, while darkness fell like fog from the air.

I glanced in my rear-view mirror. Love was keeping distance about three hundred yards behind. The pale blunt shape of his Cord loomed like a luminous coffin nose in the dying day. I looked down at the clock on my dashboard. Eight fifteen.

I switched on the huge Ducellier headlamps, and their beams bored amber tunnels for moths and midges to dance in. Here and there, on either side of the road, empty stone houses stood on the edge of vineyards or fields of sugar cane. Then the land on my right fell away into a gaping ravine, while the rock wall soared up on my left. The road had a thin strip of grey gravel on the right so that it made my tyres rumble in warning of my nearness to the edge whenever I took a corner too widely.

Suddenly, it was not cool but cold, and I was grateful for the warmth of the engine. I lit a cheroot, automatically checked oil pressure, temperature and fuel, and then changed down for the first of the bad hairpins. We were climbing steadily all the while, going up into the foothills; my car's altimeter registered 4,000 feet.

I glanced behind me once more. Love's headlights were temporarily hidden by the bend, but I could see their golden glow reflected from the side of the hill.

Far beneath and behind us, miles away through the mist, the lights of some town - Venaco? Corte? - glowed dimly like a necklace of fallen stars. The wind carried a sweet smell of the herbs, like a visit to Culpeper Hall. There was no sound at all but the faint hum of my engine and tyres, and the endless rumble of the river pouring itself over boulders hundreds of feet below me.

Within seconds, all would be dark, but just for this moment there was a timelessness about the scene, blue overlaid on deeper blue. It was a peaceful landscape, but not a peaceful land. Too many people had suffered here, had been oppressed here.

It had been occupied by aliens-the Greeks and Romans, the Byzantines, the Genoese (even for two years in the late eighteenth century by the British) then by the Germans. It had been raided by vandals and Arabs, racked by brigands and bandits who had fought out their private wars while the peasants scratched their livings from the hard, reluctant earth. Nothing was easy here; the climate was both hot and cold; all the hills were highland there were rocks in every river.

I was thinking about this, and how climate and the physical conditions of a country fashion the outlook and characters of its inhabitants — just as some cars and some people go together - when I suddenly realised that the hairpin bends were almost continual; one virtually leading into the next. The road was deteriorating rapidly.

Stones sprayed out from beneath the tyres like grape-shot; the old hand-honed gears whined slightly under the constant strain. It was now quite dark. The only glow in the cockpit came from the shrouded instrument lamps. We kept climbing more steeply, and all the time. Ten or twelve miles further and then we would be on the other side of the mountains, coasting down towards

Evisa.

The road still writhed like a serpent with indigestion, but then it levelled out slightly, and I was able to drop back into third and accelerate up to forty. Suddenly, in front of me, miles ahead along, the road, I saw a flash of amber headlamps. A car was coming towards me, driving like me, on main beam, for it was better to dazzle and be dazzled than to risk going over the side of the hill into the river and the everlasting dark.

Now and then we lost each other as I went into a tight bend and a huge wall of rock came between us. Then his lights blazed up again, bigger and brighter as he raced nearer.

I wondered who he was, for he was driving behind a pair of headlamps at least as large as mine, which meant he was also probably in an old car, because modern lights are much smaller. In the late twenties or early thirties a pair of big continental lamps could weigh a hundredweight. Now, you can get a better light from a sealed-beam unit that weighs less than a packet of tea.

He was much nearer now, possibly only a mile away; perhaps even less. And, like me, he was travelling fast. But then he was coming downhill towards me, while I was still climbing.

I had a sudden uneasy feeling that he might be some mad tourist, or a drunken local in an ancient vehicle, someone unused to night driving, or else very familiar with the road, and enraged at the sight of another car on a route he always assumed would be empty after dark.

I dipped my lights to show I meant no enmity, and he dipped his immediately in response, but it was difficult to drive on the low, spread beam, and so behind one of the outcrops of rock I turned over to main beam, and when I came out and he was much nearer, I saw he had done the same.

We were now five hundred yards apart. Then four-fifty. Then four hundred. The blaze from his huge lamps was blinding, like staring into two golden searchlights. I screwed up my eyes against their brilliance and dipped my own lights, and then pulled out towards the right of the road as near as I could to the edge.

He dipped his lights immediately in reply, but to my horror he also pulled across the road. I swung sharply back towards the left, away from the precipice, and my wheels poured out a stream of gravel chips. Incredibly, the other driver also followed me to the left, so that now we were heading towards each other on a deliberate collision course.

What the hell was the man up to? He must be mad or drunk, or both, for he seemed determined to hit me. I glanced quickly out of the cockpit to the right. A row of big stones, like dinosaur's teeth, laid end to end, marked the edge of the road. Beneath them darkness and nothing else for possibly a thousand feet, and then the tops of unseen fir trees, no doubt, and the river and the boulders.

I should pass him on this dangerous side. But what if he drove into me and forced me over the edge? Surely it would be better to keep to the left, to disobey the rule of the road, but at least give myself a fighting chance of survival? If I went over the edge and, against all odds, survived, I could lie out there all night before anyone even noticed a car had gone off the road. I slowed down. If I was going to hit him head on, the slower I was going, the better chance I would have.

Two hundred and fifty yards now. Two hundred. One-fifty. I blew my horns, and flicked my lights on and off, frantically trying to attract his attention.

Was he blind, or had he suffered a seizure - or had he been shot like Black, so that a dying or dead man's hand was on the wheel?

His lights moved like mine, deliberately copying me, baiting me. No one but a nutter would do this, or maybe someone with a grudge, who knew the road while I was a stranger.

Could Bonheur be driving towards me, intent on prising me off the road to almost certain death? The thought made my back damp with sweat. I would have to be careful-and as cunning as he appeared to be. Clearly, there was not going to be room for two of us on the road; I was determined there would be room for me.

Slowly, I eased the car over from the right of the road, away from the drop. Maybe there would be some passing space - the mouth of a quarry, the entrance to a cave, or even only a wider stretch of road where we could pass.

Seventy-five yards. Fifty. Forty. I went down through the gears into bottom, and swung the wheel over still more. The Rolls swerved sharply to the left. To my horror, the other driver, pulled over, too, just as sharply.

I jumped on my brakes. The huge tyres bit hard into the road. Stones poured out from under them like bullets. I smelted the hot bitter stench of burning rubber, the sharp acridity of smoking brake-shoes as the huge car swayed first to the left, then to the right.

He was also braking late, like me, his car also swinging from side to side under the strain, the great lamps now blinding me, now throwing their yellow beams out over the precipice or up against the rock face.

We had both left our reactions too late. Nothing could stop us hitting each other. As I slowed to a standstill, I switched off the engine in case of fire after the certain head-on impact, and threw myself sideways across the passenger seat.

Old cars don't have safety belts, and I didn't fancy my face going through all that expensive glass in the windscreen. I held my breath, body braced for the frontal blow, the jarring of heavy metal, the sickening shock of collision.

But nothing happened.

I released my. breath slowly and counted three. Still nothing happened. The other driver had switched off his engine, too. The only sounds were the thump of my heart, some mosquitoes whining in the darkness, beyond our four headlights that blazed at each other, almost bulb to bulb, and the distant rumble of the river. In the distance, I heard the big Stentor horns on Love's Cord blow their musical fanfare. It was good to know that he would be along soon, that I would not be alone with this crazy driver.

I swung myself up. Only feet away, the other car's giant headlamps blazed into mine. I could see the outline of his vehicle. Incredibly, it was a Rolls, and the same colour as mine.

'Who the hell are you?' I shouted angrily. 'What are you playing at? Are you bloody drunk?'

There was no answer. I could hear the beat of Cord's exhaust .coming up behind me now, only several hundred yards away, but still out of sight, its amber headlamps probing faintly around the hidden bends. I switched out my lights. The other driver did the same. Our four filaments died redly behind their huge lenses. I jumped down into the road, blinking in the unaccustomed darkness.

'What's happening?' I asked.

No one answered my question. I stood, one hand on my car's warm bonnet, peering to see who was in front of me. Dimly, I made out another man also standing by the side of his car, hand on the bonnet.

Then I heard a sharp intake of breath behind me, and an elbow was round my neck like a chain. A fist punched my right kidney, and I was pressed back, gasping in pain, sobbing for air.

And then the whole cliff came down on my head, and there was nothing but a loud ringing of many bells, and then darkness, and strange stars going on and off like bright neon signs in my brain.

CHAPTER NINE

I was lying on the ground, my wrists tied behind my back, my ankles bound with a leather strap which I recognised as a luggage strap from my own car.

I scrabbled my fingers and they rasped rough rock-dust. I must be in a quarry. At least it was better than a grave.

Jason Love lay about six feet away from me. His hands and feet were also tied. He was still unconscious, and blood had dried under his nose and down his chin.

I moved myself very cautiously. It was just as well, because my head jumped right off my body and took some time deciding whether to come back again. When it did return, I still had no idea where we were.

The smell of thyme sweetened the air, and against the rim of the quarry the sky was growing light. I could see my Rolls and Love's Cord parked neatly side by side, and inside the quarry, against a far wall of reddish rock, stood a shabby Fiat van.

I had seen it before, but where? My business teaches me to remember vehicles and their numbers, but my head was so' sore it took me some minutes before I could recall where I had seen it. Then I remembered; it had pulled out after me from outside a cafe in Catareggio. So maybe who had been driving it then had also slugged me on the head by the lake?

Four men lay in sleeping bags on the ground by the side of the van, snoring. A fifth man leaned against the van, smoking a cigarette and paring his nails with an engineer's file. I had never seen him before. I didn't particularly want to see him again, but I made a note of the face in case I did. He was fleshy and dark and unshaven, with a moustache; bristles sprouted on his chin as attractively as on a well-used lavatory brush.

I tried to call, to shout, but all I could do was whisper, 'Who are you? What's happened?'

He heard me and walked over to me. He wore denim trousers and a dark shirt, and a soft black leather belt with an automatic in it, and a row of rounds. He was like an extra from a cowboy film. He stood near me, looking down at me. I could smell his sweat, laced with garlic.

'So you're awake?' he asked. 'I thought maybe we'd hit you too hard.'

'Who are you?' I asked.

'Never mind,' he said. 'It's you we're interested in. You and this other bugger.'

He nodded towards Love, who was beginning to move slowly and heavily, like a sleeper reluctantly awaking.

'Are you English?' I asked the man.

'Of course I bloody am,' he said indignantly. 'What do you think I am, a Frog?'

'Why are we tied up? I thought the only bandits in Corsica were Corsicans.'

'You read too many tourist brochures,' he said. 'Never believe anything you read, mate.'

'I rarely do,' I admitted. 'Meantime, give me a drink.'

He went back to the van and opened the driver's door, returned with two tin mugs of water. He put one down beside Love and held the other up to my mouth. Most of the water dribbled down my chin into my shirt. It is difficult to drink with your hands tied behind your back when you are lying on the ground, but it's a lot better than not drinking at all.

I didn't know what I looked like, but I felt like one of those characters in ancient Rome who they threw to the lions; standing room only, free list suspended.

'Why are we tied up?' I said again, my voice returning as the water soaked into my dry throat, like rain into desert sand..

'So you don't get away,' the man said, reasonably enough.

Years ago, it seemed, centuries before, I had been driving on my merry way full of poetic thoughts and an excellent dinner. Now there was nowhere to go, and I was incapable of making even that distance.

'Who are you?' I asked again. 'And what do you want?'

Surely this could not be another nutter who wanted to discuss a plane that had come down in the lake?

'You'll learn,' he said, and walked back to the van. Love began to move and sat up, blinking his eyes.

'Don't ask me where you are,' I told him, 'because I don't know. But there's a tin of water by your side. If you don't knock it over.'

He reached out both hands, gripped the tin and emptied it, then tossed it to one side.

'What happened?' I asked him. He had been behind me and must have had a better view.

'I came round a bend,' he said slowly, thinking back. 'I saw you had stopped, and put your lights out, and then I saw you get out of the car and two fellows jumped down from the hillside on your back and clobbered you.

'I gripped a spanner and started to run towards you, but someone had fitted a trip wire across the road and they pulled this up tight, and that was as far as I got.'

'There was a car coming towards me,' I told him. 'Bloody great lights. When I swerved to the left, so did he. When I went to the right, he did exactly the same. I had to stop or hit him.'

'There wasn't any car,' said Love wearily. 'They'd simply hung a damned great pole across the road from two trees, with a plastic mirror on it. They rolled down this mirror, and what you saw was a reflection of your own headlights.'

'But what's the object of it all? Robbery?'

'God knows,' he said. 'You've been awake longer than me.'

'Wakee! Wakee!' I called out. I was feeling better; only minutes before I could not have called out if someone had offered me a hundred pounds; well, let's not be ridiculous; say fifty.

The other men dozing by the van now sat up suddenly, rubbing sleep from their eyes.

'Shut that bloody row!' one called angrily in English. I guessed they were all English. It was much lighter now. Surely there must be some traffic on the road? Surely some couple would drive into the quarry in their little Renault or Citroen to have a quick short back and sides, or a how's your father, and would discover us-to their annoyance but our deliverance?

Or maybe a coachload of trippers would pull off the road to ease their bursting bladders. We *must* be discovered. It would only be a matter of time. But then, I thought, all life is only a matter of time, and I had long passed the halfway mark.

I struggled to my feet and stood, swaying like a tree in a storm. The man who had brought us the water came towards me, his hand hovering near his gun like a hairy butterfly.

'If we can help you, we will,' I told him. 'But first undo these ropes.'

'Do that,' called one of the men near the van. 'They can't get far.'

They were all pulling themselves out of their sleeping bags, like worms out of chrysalises or whatever.

The gunman walked over to Love, took out a clasp knife, and cut the ropes around Love's wrists and ankles. Love rubbed his ankles to bring back the circulation. The man knelt and nicked the rope around my ankles and unbuckled the strap. I put out my hand for it.

'It's mine,' I said.

He threw it into the back of the Rolls for me.

'It's not the strap I'm after,' he said.

'Then what *are* you after?' I asked, feeling like the nut in the story who takes a girl in his car down a lonely road and then stops and asks her, 'Do you believe in the hereafter?'

And when she replies she doesn't know, he tells her: 'Well, if I don't get what I'm here after ,*you'll* be here after the car's gone.'

'Don't give me that innocence crap,' the man retorted. 'You know bloody well what's hidden in one of those cars. And I'm telling you now, before you get any wrong ideas, that you're going to tell us *where* it's hidden.'

'Where what's hidden?'

'You stupid berk,' he said disgustedly. 'Save your breath. We'll find it, if we have to take those cars apart, nut and bolt.'

'The best of luck' I said. 'But I don't know what you're talking about.'

He hit me then, suddenly, with the back of his hand across my mouth. I staggered and fell. By the time I had painfully hauled myself up again, he had walked back to the van. The other men had already rolled up their sleeping bags. One was brewing coffee on a Gaz ring. It smelled good, even at that distance. He brought over two cups, gave one to Love, and the other to me. I spat the blood out of my mouth and took the coffee gratefully.

'You are English?' Love asked the man.

'Yes.'

'So what's all this in aid of? I'm a doctor, engaged by Pagoda Films for some location work. What do you expect to gain from this hold-up?'

'This idiot' - the man jerked his head in my direction -'knows exactly where something's been hidden in one of these cars - maybe in both of them. All he's got to do is tell us where it is. Otherwise you'll both take the cars apart, bit by bit. Which could take a long time. Do I make my meaning clear?'

'Perfectly,' said Love. 'If we knew what you were talking about. But the Rolls my friend here is driving is the property of a patient's son. The Cord is mine. And there's nothing hidden in either.'

'What are you looking for?' I asked the man. It would help if we knew.

'Sparklers,' he said. 'Diamonds.'

'How can we have any diamonds hidden in the cars when we haven't got any to hide?' I asked him, reasonably enough, I thought. 'I drove the Rolls from London only a few days ago. Apart from a few short runs, it's been stuck in an hotel park ever since.'

At that moment, one of the men who had been dumping the sleeping bags in the back of the van, gave a great shout of alarm and came running towards us.

'Amsterdam!' he shouted in a panic. 'He's had a fit! He's out cold.'

The man who brought us the coffee glanced at Love.

'You a doctor of medicine?'

'Yes.'

'Then come over here and prove it.'

I followed them to the van, glad of the chance to prove I could still walk. We peered inside. On the scratched metal floor, hands tied at his wrists, lay Amsterdam. In his fawn lightweight trousers, his dark red sports shirt, he might have been a bondage fetishist taking a rest. But a second glance at his glazed face, at his eyes sightless as black-currants, showed that this was a sleep from which he would never awaken. Maybe his heart really had been bad. Either way, it didn't bother him now. Nothing ever would again. Amsterdam was dead as yesterday's news.

'What's he doing here?' I asked. 'Lying in state?'

'We brought him along,' said the gunman shortly. 'He knew about the diamonds. This van gets very hot inside. Maybe he had a stroke!'

'Or maybe you killed him?'

He didn't answer.

'How are we going to get rid of him?' asked someone eke, obviously frightened. Kidnapping was one thing; robbery, another; death, a third. A body was a big object to hide, and even in these lonely gorges the diving carrion birds would eventually draw attention to it.

'Put him at the wheel of the van,' suggested the gunman, 'and push the whole damn thing over the side. Make it look like an accident.'

'They could trace the van too easily,' someone else pointed out.

'Right,' said the gunman. 'Then let's drive the van up to the wreckers' yard and tip the body out. All those bloody hogs and boars will do the rest. They'll eat anything.'

I remembered those piles of ruined cars and the huge pigs

snouting and grouting in the mounds of rubbish. I remembered Bonheur with his rifle. I remembered a lot of things.

'How far is the yard from here?' I asked.

'Couple of hundred yards. Turn left out of the quarry and back over the hill,' said the gunman.

'When shall we do it?' asked his companion.

'Later,' said the gunman. 'Let's get these fellows working first.' He turned to me.

'Get over to that Rolls,' he said shortly. 'We'll take it first. Start dismantling.'

'What sort of container are we supposed to be looking for?' I asked.

'You know bloody well what it is, anywhere it is. So cut out the questions and get moving. Start with the front bumper and work back. Then take each wheel off and remove the tyres.'

'Let's have another coffee first,' I suggested, playing for time. The longer we were stuck the more chance there must be of someone finding us. 'It's going to be a long job.'

Another man brought over the pot of coffee and filled our cups. I walked over with mine to the Rolls. The other men followed me and stood behind.

'Give me air,' I said. 'I don't like being watched at work. Even Casanova couldn't have done a good job if he'd had ten eyeballs on him all the time.'

'Don't try anything,' said the gunman. 'If you do, you're dead. Then we'll just set light to the car and burn it out. And your body with it. We're giving you a chance.'

I unlocked the torpedo-shaped tool box on the left of the car, and took out a roll of ring spanners, each beautifully silver-plated in the traditional Rolls way.

'Don't hang about, buster,' warned the gunman irritably. 'There's no chance of anyone coming in here to rescue you, if that's what you're hoping for. We've strung a pole across the entrance with a sign Keep Out. Explosives. Blasting.'

'You think of everything,' said Love sadly.

'All the important things.'

'Then I'd better start on my car.'

'Follow him,' said the gunman.

Two men detached themselves and walked behind Love to the Cord. He opened the driver's door, lifted up the front seat, and from the tool box underneath it also took out a handful of spanners. He laid them out neatly, in order of size, like a surgeon's instruments, on the bonnet top.

'Where shall we start?' he asked.

'Front bumper. Like your friend.'

I tapped the Rolls' bumper. It rang like a bell.

'There's nothing inside. You can see it's just a strip of metal,' I told the gunman. He grunted disbelievingly, but was forced to accept the obvious.

'Take the lamps apart then,' he ordered.

I began to unscrew the huge, plated rims of the head-lights. The sun was moving up the sky. Already, I could feel a trickle of sweat running down behind my shoulder-blades. I glanced up, across the patrician radiator, beyond the silver lady, through the windscreen, towards Love.

The Cord bumper was also only a thin strip of metal, and Love had progressed beyond it into the engine compartment. The heavy blunt coffin-nosed bonnet was open. Hinged at the back-the first car to have such a bonnet, incidentally-and supported on its single stay, it looked like an alligator's mouth, hungry snapping jaws held apart by a thin stick.

I heard Love suddenly call out excitedly to one of the men: 'Is *that* what you are looking for?'

'What?' asked the first man.

The gunman looked up, eyes narrowed, head on one side, instantly alert.

'That box down behind the solenoid,' said Love.

'Where's the solenoid?'

'There. That round thing.'

Love bent more deeply into the great open mouth of the car,

pointing out what he had discovered.

'I don't know,' said the man uneasily. He had no idea either what shape the package would be.

'Well, what do *you* think?' asked Love, turning to the second man. 'That's the box, down there.'

Both men were now leaning over the horizontal louvres of the bonnet, peering at what Love had pointed out to them. Love called over to the man with the gun.

'There's something here,' he said. 'You'd better have a look yourself. It's going to be difficult to remove.'

The gunman began to walk slowly towards the Cord, his hand for the first time not near his pistol. He had reached the side of my door, when Love suddenly ducked, pushed the bonnet's retaining stay, and dropped to the ground.

Two hundredweight of curved metal bonnet, sharp as a guillotine, came down on the backs of the bowed men. They screamed in pain and surprise as it bit through their shirts into their flesh. Their feet scuffed dust in an agony of energy as they struggled desperately to be free, but they could not move because their shoulders and their arms' were pinned beneath the bonnet. Its weight held them prisoner as tightly as the jaws of a man trap.

Their cries and moans grew fainter, and their feet stopped running on the spot as the pain spread, and they sank into unconsciousness.

The gunman fired. His bullet stirred a trail of dust at Love's feet. Love had jumped behind the body of the nearest man. The gunman slowly lowered his pistol. To shoot Love would mean shooting him, too.

The gunman gave a sudden leap to the left, meaning to shoot Love from the side. I was still holding a screwdriver in my hand. I also leapt to the left, jumped on the gunman's back and drove the blade right up his jack. For a second, I felt resistance, then the sharp end was through the cloth of his trousers and his underpants and right up his fundamental orifice. He screamed, then fired wildly in a reflex action. I counted the shots. As he fired his sixth and last, I shouted, *'Now!'*

Love ran from the Cord and trod his gun hand into the ground. The fingers opened, but Love could not pick up the gun, for the other two men were on us. One kicked Love in the groin as he bent for the gun, and then brought down a spanner on his head.

The second man kicked me in the face, and I let go of the gunman and rolled over to one side.

For a long moment there was nothing but pain, and the sound of our grunting, and the moaning of the gunman as he crawled on all fours with a bloodstained screwdriver sticking through the back of his trousers, like a wooden-handled tail.

'You bastards,' said one of the new arrivals. He held us covered by a pistol, moving it first towards Love's head, then to mine, as we, lay.

His companion ran to the Cord and opened the bonnet. The two men slid out and lay on their backs writhing slightly, like turtles in the dust.

'Now, I'll shoot you lot as you lie,' said the gunman. 'Where it will hurt the most.'

Anger had thinned his lips. His face was a gargoyle mask of rage. I could see him silhouetted against the deepening blue of the sky. A few scuds of cloud moved by miles away, quite unconcerned, in an entirely different world.

I could see the bright green myrtle plants and yellow gorse bobbing in the morning breeze. I saw all this with an astonishing sharpness and intensity because I believed I would never see anything again; and as Dr. Johnson remarked on another, less violent, occasion, there's nothing to concentrate a man's mind better than the knowledge that he's going to hang.

'If you shoot,' said Love levelly, 'then you'll never find what you are looking for.'

'Balls,' said the nearest man. 'We'll just set fire to these bloody heaps, and then we'll find it a damn sight quicker than with you.'

He raised his pistol to take aim, pointing at me. I could see skin grow white over his knuckles as he squeezed the trigger. He wore a gold ring with a red stone on his right little finger. I watched this, rather than see his first finger crook and tighten on the trigger.

'This is it, then,' he said softly.

The finger moved almost imperceptibly. My heart literally stopped beating. This *was* it, then. The end of the chapter. Death.

And then, suddenly, inexplicably, amazingly, his finger relaxed and his hand opened and he gave a sobbing cry, and the pistol spun out of his grasp and dropped in the dust at my feet.

My heart started to beat again. The man was bent double, pressing his right elbow into his groin in an extremity of pain, and where his fingers had been there was now only a bloody mass of raw flesh and pink, splintered bone.

I looked up behind him, beyond the edge of the quarry. Three men were coming down the hills, walking slowly, smiling. They wore blue jeans and sweat-shirts and they moved silently and in step in their rubber-soled boots.

The first carried a rifle with a telescopic sight under his arm, not as a sportsman or an amateur carries a gun, but as a pro carries one. It was part of his body - an extension of his own bone, a piece of his own mind. I recognised him without the slightest difficulty. Bonheur.

A man I had never seen before walked behind him, chewing a blade of grass. The third man, with his black leather belt hung with cartridges for the Mauser he held in his right hand, was Jean-Paul.

I crawled up on all fours, and then stood upright. The gun lay on the ground in front of me. This somehow didn't seem the moment to pick it up. The three men were against the sun, and my eyes were watering with pain and dust and weariness, and for a hundred other reasons.

'A little trouble, yes?' asked the stranger gently, like a hotel receptionist enquiring whether we liked our rooms.

'You could call it that,' agreed Love. '

Bonheur walked over to the two men by the Cord and stood

looking down on them. He hawked in his throat and spat in the first one's face. Then he filled his mouth with more saliva and spat in the second man's face. He was a good spitter; he hit both targets.

'Friends of yours?' I asked him.

He smiled sourly.

'The vanquished have no friends. Only the victors.'

'You're a philosopher then?' asked Love, trying to keep the conversation going. Hadn't Churchill once declared that jaw-jaw was better than war-war?

'A realist,' Bonheur replied.

'So what are you being realistic about now?' I asked him.

Jean-Paul crossed over to me.

'You know damned well what I am being realistic about. What these fellows want. The diamonds.'

'There *are* no diamonds,' I said wearily. Maybe if I told the truth often enough someone, given time and a grain of intelligence, would believe me.

'Maybe the good Dr. Love knows, then?'

Love said nothing. He was also standing up slowly, as though to move too swiftly would be fatal. I felt much the same way; we had only exchanged one set of masters for another.

'Where did they come from, these bloody diamonds everyone seems to want?' I asked Bonheur. 'First, you take me to some mad, blind old aristo who chases me around a darkened house, asking me questions about a plane that I can't answer. Then you try to shoot me off his roof. Next, these characters ambush me, and *now you* turn up as the rescuer.

'One day you're the dragon, the next you're St. George. You should decide on your role and stick with it.'

'It is really very simple,' said Jean-Paul, as though speaking to idiot children.

'These gentlemen who ambushed you so crudely in a territory that for generations has gone under the control of the Vicomte's family are, as you know, countrymen of yours - Englishmen.

'A few weeks ago, they organised a very sophisticated robbery at an international diamond-exhibition in Hong Kong. They got away with two million pounds' worth of sparklers.'

Standing there, dusty head aching, sweat streaming down my neck, I remembered another morning, one in my garage, when George was fitting a new leather bellows to an old S.U. pump, and I'd heard the news of the theft on my transistor, along with other items that had meant no more to me. But that was then; this was now.

'But then things started to go wrong. Big things. Black was to land in England, hand over the sparklers to our injured friend here' - Jean-Paul nodded towards the gunman, now squatting on his hams, gripping his shattered hand as though this could somehow cure the wound - 'then take off immediately, and re-land officially at a registered airport, go through customs and so on.

'But a cross wind blew him off course. He took a short cut over the Vicomte's land - and the Vicomte brought him down.

'The plane sank in the Etang, but Black parachuted out and got back safely to England. However, he had missed his rendezvous and did not know how to contact the people who should have met him - or even who they were. And, let's be fair, he didn't make much effort. Instead, he put up a proposition to Amsterdam.

'For a cut of whatever the jewels fetched, Amsterdam agreed to pretend to make a film involving a boat chase. He meant to sink one boat, and then someone could go down, apparently to salvage it, but, in fact, to take the diamonds out of the plane. But he didn't dare risk having Black with him in case some of the other side knew him. This annoyed Black. Understandably. He thought Amsterdam was trying to cut him out, so he came over here on his own.'

He paused. I had a sudden recollection of the lake, silver under the moon, and two heads bobbing as the divers surfaced. Amsterdam must have been after the diamonds then-but had he found them?

'They both reckoned without the Vicomte's natural interest in who - or what - he had shot down. We were the Vicomte's ears and eyes. We listened and we watched. When you and Black were to start going round and round in your boats, we realised you could be there indefinitely, for there were no crew and no cameras.

'So I decided to stand down when Black offered me a thousand francs to show how well he could drive a boat, and my friend, Bonheur here, precipitated things by shooting him.'

'He could just as easily have shot you,' Jean-Paul said to me. 'As it happened, he shot Black, which gave Amsterdam an instant excuse to start diving, without any questions being asked.

'We expected that the original thieves would work out, by a process of elimination, roughly where the plane had come down - and then ambush whoever they thought had collected the diamonds. And we were proved right. It is always easier to let other people do the hard work. I must say, they have done that most effectively.'

'But not successfully,' I said. 'They still haven't found the diamonds.'

'*I* know where they are,' said Love quietly.

'What?' I said, astonished.

'There is a time for silence, and a time for speech,' Love said sonorously. 'As these gentlemen have saved our lives, I will help them find the diamonds.'

I looked at Love in amazement. Was he doing a Harpic-going right round the bend? What kind of Napoleonic rubbish was this?

Love looked at me, and his face seemed as serene and solemn as a judge putting someone down for ten years for flashing it during daylight hours from the third tree on the left as you enter Hyde Park.

I closed my eyes, trying to imagine I was elsewhere, but I couldn't close my ears. I heard Love boom on like a man boring for England.

'I will have to ask that you *all* come with me to this van. And, then, secondly, that we do so with bared heads, to show respect for the dead. As we are now, so once was he.'

'Who?' asked Jean-Paul.

'Amsterdam.'

'Is he dead, then?'

'Yes.'

Love picked up his medical bag from his car.

'Follow me,' he told them. 'But first tie up these characters.'

He nodded towards the two Englishmen; the gunman didn't count anyway. Bonheur and Jean-Paul had ropes round their wrists and ankles before Love had finished speaking. They lay trussed like supermarket chickens, and just as harmless.

The three Corsicans set off behind Love at a smart pace; nobody bothered about me. I followed twenty feet behind them.

The van's paint had powdered under several summers of sun and it was covered with reddish dust; flies and wasps were buzzing greedily around the rear doors.

Love opened one of these doors and beckoned Jean-Paul and the other man inside. He followed them in. Bonheur stayed outside with me.

'Hats off, gentlemen,' ordered Love, briskly. 'A mark of respect.'

He nodded towards me.

'Take them, please.'

I came up to the door, and took the three black felt hats. The bands felt damp and greasy with sweat; they smelt of lavender hair oil. It was like a ponces' reunion.

'I will need your help', Love went on. 'Mr. Amsterdam was a large man in life, and in death he is not diminished. You must help me to move him on a stretcher up to the far end of the van.'

'Why?' asked Jean-Paul. 'The fact he's dead is no concern of ours.'

'It should be very much your concern,' retorted Love sharply.

'If you must have it spelled out, he has the diamonds on his person.'

'Let's get them off his person, then.'

'Exactly. But first we have to get him in a position so we *can* remove them,' explained Love more patiently. 'Do you wish to get them, or don't you?'

'Of course.'

Love was nearer to the open door. He bent down and opened his medical bag.

'What are you doing?' asked Bonheur, his eyes narrowing with suspicion.

'Gentlemen, I have to make an autopsy on the dead.'

'You mean cut Amsterdam open?' asked Jean-Paul in surprise.

'Yes.'

'You mean . . .' Jean-Paul swallowed.

'The diamonds, gentlemen, are in his stomach. He has swallowed them. One by one. Each is encased in a resinous coat, so they would not cut his intestinal wall.'-

Love glanced briefly at his watch.

'Since by my calculations he would have swallowed them yesterday evening, it is impossible to say whether they will still be in his stomach or in his bowel. I must warn you that the operation will be messy and disagreeable. Especially in this heat.'

The three Corsicans looked at each other uneasily. The van felt hot as an oven; sweat was already streaming down their faces, and dark streaks of it stained their shirts. The smell of death was sweet and sickly: soon it would become putrefying. A few flies were marking time around Amsterdam's nose and mouth. His eyes stared up at the roof, seeing nothing.

'Come on,' said Love impatiently.

'You, sir,' He turned ,to Jean-Paul 'You take the shoulders. Now, you at the middle,' he pointed to the next man, 'and you, Monsieur Bonheur, at the feet. Move him farther down inside the van.'

They bent reluctantly to their task, while Love rummaged in

his bag. I could see the packets of drugs, the round boxes of pills and two syringes in a nickel-plated case, and a square leather box the size of a large cigar packet. He opened this. Inside, scalpels and separate surgical blades glittered sharp as shark's teeth.

'This will not be pleasant, gentlemen,' said Love bluntly. 'Nor will it be quick. These diamonds could be anywhere in something like twenty-eight feet of intestine. And we will have to examine every inch - as well, of course, as the contents of the stomach.

'I suggest you may care to remove your shirts. Sometimes there is an accumulation of gas in a dead body. And fluids can spurt out, leaving unpleasant stains and smells that are difficult to remove from clothing.'

Jean-Paul and the stranger looked at each other and pulled off their shirts.

'Give them to me,' I said. They handed them across Amsterdam's corpse. I rolled them into a bundle.

Bonheur still stood uneasily by the door, crossing himself in a strange, belatedly religious way. I had a little personal business to settle with Bonheur. This seemed to be as good a moment as any for conducting it.

'Do you need Monsieur Bonheur with you?' I asked Love. He glanced at me over Bonheur's head, a brief flicker of understanding in his eyes.

'I think he is possibly feeling unwell,' he said. 'Are you not, Bonheur?'

The man nodded. The presence of death is disquieting for many people, especially and ironically those who like to call others to eternity before their time.

'Then take him out. I cannot have squeamish people around me as I operate.'

'Come outside,' I told Bonheur. 'You will feel better in the shade.'

He leaned against the side of the van, half sitting on the rear mudguard, thankful to be out of that cramped tin box, sweet with the smell of death, and the horrible prospect of who knew what desecration.

I returned to the open door of the van. Love handed me his own shirt and pulled on a pair of pink rubber gloves. The other two men stood waiting on the far side of Amsterdam's body. Love flicked his fingers in annoyance as though he had just remembered something.

'I'd better disinfect the air first. Germs from the dead, gentlemen, can be extremely virulent. Millions are breeding every second in this corpse. Sometimes they are fatal. So breathe deeply with this aerosol.'

Love took a few deep breaths himself. The others followed his example. Then he bent down into his bag and pulled out a small grey cylinder the size of a half-pint milk bottle, with a tap and a gauge at one end. I saw that he held his breath as he turned on this tap. Then he began to talk, slowly, persuasively.

'Keep breathing, gentlemen. More strongly, please. This is the strongest disinfectant in the world. It will kill or neutralise all known bacteria. And it is essential you completely fill your lungs.'

For a second, Jean-Paul and the other man stood, breathing in and out slowly, hands at their sides, and then, almost at the same moment, they keeled over across Amsterdam. Their legs turned to rubber and they slid limply to the floor.

Love tossed the gas cylinder inside, grabbed his bag and jumped out of the van. He slammed the door shut behind him and leaned against it for a second, letting out his breath.

'Nitrous oxide-laughing gas. The joke's on them for a change.'

'What do you mean?' asked Bonheur, and brought his rifle up across his body, all nausea gone under the impetus of sudden and unexpected danger..

'This,' I said, and threw the bundle of shirts in his face. His left hand instinctively went up to ward them off and I kicked him in the crotch, hard.

He fired the rifle. The bullet buried itself in the hot, dry stone-dust. He started to run, limping in his pain, reloading as he ran, and from twenty yards away, he turned and fired again, twice. I felt my left arm jump without any instructions from me, and looked down at my sleeve. A patch of red had suddenly appeared on the cloth. I dropped down on my hands and knees, threw a handful of small stones at him with my right hand. They all missed. He went on running, and I went after him.

'Wait!' shouted Love. 'He's hit you.'

'I know that,' I said. 'I'll wait when I've got him.'

I could still move the fingers of my left hand, but a dull ache was spreading up towards my shoulder. I pushed my hand into my shirt front and ran on, like a left-handed Napoleon.

Bonheur was increasing the distance between us. He used his rifle butt as a stick to help him climb the almost sheer wall of the quarry. Showers of stone and dust poured down as he struggled up and was over into the gorse and myrtle. I came up behind him more slowly. My heart was pounding like an old side-valve engine on a long hill when the ignition's too retarded.

The ground was flat above the quarry, and I got some breath back here. Then it dipped and rose again, and on the breast of the hill I could see the familiar blue and red and grey shapes of the cars in the wrecker's yard. Bonheur obviously had some kind of a hideout here. Anyway, he would be safe behind all that metal. He would be safe in any case, I thought bitterly, for I had no gun.

He ran on steadily, now and then glancing back at me. I ran on more slowly, sweat pouring down into my eyes. He was about fifty yards ahead when he vaulted the wire fence and disappeared among the cars. I did not cross the fence behind him in case he had a bead on it, but went over about thirty yards to the right. Then I bent down and picked a huge gear wheel out of the dust and tossed it over the top of a pyramid of Simcas and Citroens. It landed on a metal roof that boomed like a giant gong.

Bonheur's rifle cracked twice. The bullets whanged off a door somewhere, harmless as castrated bees. He had fired six shots already. His magazine was unlikely to hold more than ten, and he had no bandolier. I crept down an alley between car doors that swung and creaked above me, wondering what I could do to swing the pendulum of advantage my way.

Through the wire fence, the hogs were raising streaming snouts and peering through tiny red eyes at this unexpected activity. Hardly any of them were eating. That meant they had nothing left to eat, which meant again that they would be hungry. Possibly the refuse lorries were due very soon.

Thirty or forty of the beasts were crowding along the wire now, their blunt, sawn-off noses streaming with rheum, yellow tusks fouled, lips pink and slobbery in expectation of food. Even in my situation, I shuddered. I was very glad of the wire between us. If they rushed me and got me down, maddened by the sight and smell of blood, I would never stand up again.

I held my breath and listened. I could hear nothing but rusty hinges creaking, and the scream of some carrion birds squabbling among the rubbish.

I threw a connecting rod and then a hub cap into the mass of car bodies. Both banged away on unseen bonnets and roofs. Bonheur fired twice. Two still to go. Where the hell was he hiding in all this maze of ancient vehicles?

I peered cautiously round a corner, sheltering behind the rusting hulk of a Chevrolet convertible, all fins and chromium beading.

At the far end of the cars, behind a Renault without any windows, but giving him the protection of two doors against my bullets, if I'd got any, I could see Bonheur crouched with his rifle, head cocked on one side, listening. I drew back. We could play this game all day, or until the refuse men arrived, and then who would they believe - the Corsican they knew, or a foreigner, wounded, unshaven, and obviously on the run? I *must* take the initiative before others seized it for me. But how?

I crawled backwards to the first alley, desperate for a plan, even an idea. The sun was now moving steadily up the sky, and the heat, reflected and amplified by so much metal, made me realise how dry my mouth was. Worse, my left arm was throbbing now as though it had a private heart of its own. Never mind; I had my own doctor only a few hundred yards away. But first I had to get even with Bonheur. More important, I had not forgotten the Bucciali and the Voisin which, under the Vicomte's will, now belonged to him. He held the key to my life - and a profit, both very dear to me.

I knelt on the ground for another look at him, and something sharp pressed into my right knee like a goad. I put down my hand and pulled away a small metal hook, the end of an elastic strap from part of an octopus.

Months ago, or maybe even only weeks before, this strap had helped to secure some suitcase on a roof rack for a family off on holiday. I fed it slowly through my fingers. It was about two feet long and the other end was frayed, with five or six thin strands of black rubber poking out of the red and green canvas covering.

I stared at it, not really seeing it, then suddenly I realised I had found my weapon. I rummaged in the grey dust, among the shoots of grass, until I found an aluminium strip and bent this into a V. It was the kick-plate from under the door of some long-forgotten car, and it had half-a-dozen screw holes bored in it. Through one of these I pushed the hook, and then drew the elastic tight and tied the other end to the second arm of the V.

I now had a crude catapult. I grouted about like a two-legged hog until I found half-a-dozen wheel nuts for ammunition and then I began to crawl cautiously along between the cars, nearer the Renault where Bonheur was hiding.

I came to a gap between a Peugeot station wagon and a Dodge truck down on its brake drums, and squeezed between them, holding my breath until, through the ventilating louvres of the Dodge bonnet, I could see the Renault and Bonheur still behind it.

He was licking his lips nervously. His mouth must be as dry as mine. I stood up quickly and fired my first wheel nut slightly to his right. I just had time to see it dent a door before I dropped. He fired his rifle, but not at my target, because he did not know what had hit the door.

I sent off a second nut and a third. He fired again. I let go a fourth wheel nut. And then I listened. Over the thunder of my own heart, I heard the faint, harmless click of a rifle bolt. He was out of rounds.

I stood up now, holding the aluminium strip painfully in my left hand, for I had more strength in my right to draw back the elastic. I slipped a nut into the sling and pulled the rubber as far as it would come, until the metal V began to bend. Then I released it.

The wheel nut missed Bonheur's head, where I'd aimed, but hit him in the chest.

Bonheur fell back, not knowing what had struck him. And in that instant of bewilderment, I ran to him. As he writhed on his back, I kicked him in the guts, pulled the rifle out of his hands and swung it like a club.

'Get up, you bastard,' I ordered.

He struggled to his feet. I didn't know whether he had another gun or a knife, but I threw his rifle away behind me, and reloaded my sling with a wheel nut.

'You tried to shoot me when I was on the roof of the Vicomte's house,' I began.

He said nothing.

'You also shot Black. But you *meant* to get me, didn't you?'

'It was a mistake, monsieur,' he said. His voice was hoarse, only a whisper, as though he was speaking against a strong wind. 'I thought *you* were in charge.'

'I am now.'

'What do you want?' he asked.

'Two things,' I told him. 'First, I gave you a hundred franc tip. I want that back. I don't tip for bad service!'

A look of amazement crossed his face. One of his hands began to go towards an inside jacket pocket.

'Don't try anything,' I warned, 'or I'll kill you. I'm a good, shot with this sling.'

I wasn't, but he was in no position to argue. He took out a wallet, removed a hundred franc note, rolled it into a ball and threw it to me. I caught it and put it in my own back pocket.

Then I put my left hand inside my jacket, brought out a Biro and threw it at him. He caught it clumsily. I bent down and picked up a discarded piston, crammed a sheet of paper from my diary into this and threw that at him, too.

'Now you can write,' I said, 'without putting your hands anywhere near your pockets.' I was speaking more slowly. My wound was proving more painful. I felt lightheaded; the sun was uncomfortably hot.

'Write this. I, Charles Bonheur, as at this date, give and bequeath the two vintage motor cars, the Bucciali and the Voisin, left to me under the will of the late Vicomte de Venaco, to Aristo Autos, Belgravia Mews, London, England.'

He wrote laboriously spinning out the business, knowing that while he wrote I would not kill him.

'Sign it,' I ordered.

'You need a witness,' replied Bonheur suddenly.

'God is my witness,' I said. 'Now throw it back.'

He put the Biro mechanically into his own breast pocket and I didn't remind him it was mine. It was hard enough to catch the piston and extract the note.

'Now what are you going to do?' he asked dully.

'Give you a chance,' I told him. 'First, come out from that car.'

He walked round the side of the Renault slowly, his eyes flickering like lizards' tongues, desperate for a weapon and a chance of escape.

'Keep in the middle between the cars,' I said. 'If you try anything, I'll kill you.'

He backed up against the wire.

'Climb over the wire,' I ordered him.

'No,' he said hoarsely. 'Not with those boars. They're wild. They'll kill me.'

'Not if you don't panic, they won't.'

He was pressed right up against the wire fence now, and the animals, attracted by our voices, were surging impatiently in a greedy scabrous tide of swollen backs and wet grunting snouts and tossing tusks.

Bonheur suddenly glanced at them, ducked, seized a half shaft from the ground and threw it at me. I dropped down on my hands and knees to avoid it and he leapt at me. I let go of the elastic. At six feet range I could hardly miss, and I didn't.

The nut hit him in the forehead, just where David hit Goliath, and with the same dramatic effect. He fell, semi-stunned, then he began to crawl feebly, like an animal, desperate to escape.

I heard the wire crack as the hungry boars, excited by the action, by the sight of a human who walked upright on two legs, now down on the ground like them, surged against the fence. The posts snapped like twigs. Then the grey stinking tide of foulness was in among the cars with us, the earth trembling with the gross weight of their swollen bodies, some so huge and fat they dragged their bellies on the ground. I turned and ran. And when I heard Bonheur shouting and screaming behind me I did not look back. After all, he had a chance. The boars might be vegetarians.

'Bonjour, Bonheur,' I said to myself. 'Next time, treat a stranger like a friend. He might be another car dealer.'

I didn't hear him answer. I didn't hear anything as I climbed down shakily to the quarry. I didn't want to listen. Love was leaning against his Cord, smoking a cigar as though nothing had happened, and maybe not a lot had in world terms or in his.

I held out my left arm. He rolled up the sleeve, opened his medical bag, bound up the wound. He asked nothing about Bonheur and I told him nothing, either. Then he opened the boot of the Cord, took out a white wooden case with a red cross painted on the lid and stamped: FIRST AID: OPEN ONLY ON DR. LOVE'S INSTRUCTIONS.

Presumably, he was instructing himself, for he unlocked it with a small silver key. Inside lay two bottles of red wine and two glasses in specially shaped felt-lined recesses. He took a corkscrew from the lid and drew one cork. We had a glass of wine each.

'For medicinal purposes only,' he said gravely.

'Of course,' I replied, just as grave. Actually, there wasn't a lot to laugh about, but I wasn't crying, either. Not with Bonheur's paper in my pocket. Monsieur Rossi would have another client soon. I thought we would understand each other.

Love replaced the bottle and glasses and locked up the box.

'Let's go,' he said, and we went. As we climbed into our cars one of the Englishmen shouted out desperately: 'You're not leaving us, are you?'

'Regrettably, yes,' replied Love. 'But you will not be lonely for long. We'll do our best to see you have visitors shortly. You have my word for that.'

'And mine,' I said, and added, for good measure, a touch of the old Français. *'Merde.'*

Love started his engine and drew level with me.

'What about Victoria?' he asked. 'Shall we head for Ajaccio and pick her up there?'

'We'll pick her up long before then.'

'How do you know?'

'Because, doctor, I take a less idealistic view of human nature than many in your profession. I believe most people are bastards, although they sometimes lack the courage to exploit their natural illegitimacy to the full.

'On all my old cars I fit a small reserve tank under the chassis. When I park the cars, I switch on a hidden magnetic tap. So if anyone drives them off without any knowledge they can only drive so far.

'I think Victoria's probably gone so far. I'd say she'll be stuck a few miles on up the road.'

We came over the top of a hill, and there at the bottom, parked half on the road, half off, was the boat-tailed Rolls. Victoria had obviously run out of petrol on the crest of the hill and had freewheeled down to the bottom, a distance of five or six miles.

I could imagine her throwing the clutch in and out desperately in frantic attempts to start the engine, and all the while the fuel gauge, connected to the main tank, would be reading reassuringly high. She would assume that the fault was something dire, and no doubt she had set off to walk or hitch a lift to the nearest garage, perhaps ten or fifteen miles ahead.

We pulled over in front of the Rolls, and climbed out. The sun was right up the sky now. Love opened the boot of the Cord, and took out the wooden case again. We sat down in the sun on the bank, amid the whirring crickets with the smell of the maquis sweetening the wind, glasses in our hands and followed St. Paul's advice, to take a little wine for our stomachs' sakes.

A car came up and over the hill behind us. It slowed and then stopped, seeing our three antiques parked one behind the other. It was a little English Imp, with a middle-aged couple inside; the driver in blue open-necked shirt and shorts; the woman with those soft, puffy arms that come with middle age. A few greying tendrils that had escaped her husband's blunt razor peered out from under her armpits. Maybe someone had loved her once, long ago.

'Can we help you?' the man asked, reassured by our English number plates and the GB discs on the back of our cars.

'Yes, indeed,' said Love. He turned to me. 'I'd better ring the police and explain what has happened up the road.'

'Has there been an accident?' asked the woman hopefully, her dull mean eyes flitting from the cars to us. Her life was so dreary that any prospect became an adventure. I could imagine her at home: the semi-detached house, *Mon Repos,* or *Casa Mia.* The budgerigar under a sheet in its cage, while the husband watched the box in carpet slippers, and filtered cocoa through his moustache, wondering where his life had gone.

'I'll hitch a lift if I may,' Love went on.

'Delighted,' said the man. 'Move over, Madge and let him in.'

I thought, meanly, how gallant. It must have been a long time since someone had taken advantage of such an offer.

I watched the little car shimmer out of sight in the distance, and I. poured myself some more wine, wondering what the others would say to the police when they arrived to discover two men tied up, three wounded, and two more locked in with a corpse.

Then I thought of other things, for I heard a truck grinding up the hill in low gear. It was an old Citroen with a breakdown crane on the back. The driver pulled in ahead of me. He was a huge man with an Aertex vest, and hair curling out at me like black wire through the holes.

He hadn't shaved for days and his eyes were shot with blood, red as bicycle reflectors. Victoria jumped down from the cab, astonished at seeing me, bottle in hand.

'Where's the breakdown?' asked the Frog.

'Nowhere,' I said. 'There's been a mistake.'

'What do you mean?' asked Victoria. 'The Rolls won't start, yet there's petrol and a spark and everything.'

'How much do I owe you?' I asked the driver, ignoring her technical stuff.

He looked at Victoria, trying to get her thin dress against the sun to see what pants she wore, if she wore any.

'Five hundred francs,' he said quickly.

'How much?' I repeated, frowning, holding the wine bottle like an Indian club.

'Four hundred,' he said defensively.

'I'm a bit deaf.'

'Three fifty,' he said sullenly.

I handed him the money He climbed back into his truck, rolled a cigarette, spat out of the window into the thyme, reversed and went back over the hill. The road burned emptily under the hard hot sun.

'So you found me,' said Victoria brightly.

I stood looking at her, wine in my hand. I didn't offer her any.

'Yes,' I agreed. 'I found you. You didn't expect that, did you?'

'Well, I thought we'd meet in Ajaccio.'
'That would have been too late.'
'For what?'
'You bloody well know for what,' I said. 'And I don't mean a bit of the old how's your father. I've been beaten up by two sets of people, nearly murdered by a blind madman, shot at from the top of a roof - and you, of all people, know for what and for why.'

The wine was fuming away inside me now; I always get verbose when I drink in the heat of the day. I should drink then more often.

I walked over to her Alpine, bent down under the running board, put my secret key into the electric lock and turned it. Then I climbed up behind the wheel, switched on the ignition, waited until the petrol pumps stopped pattering away, and pressed the starter. The huge old engine swung into instant life. Then I switched off.

'I've never driven this car,' I said thoughtfully.
'Well, what about that?'

I was thinking about that. And about that evening in the mews when Black visited me, when the engine had been hastily cleaned; when my tools had been moved, and there was a smell of hasty work in the garage; about the time I had offered to drive it into Venaco, but Victoria had found an excuse to stop me; about the way the Alpine had lagged behind when we drove in convoy from Ajaccio.

I got out, opened the bonnet, and ran my hand along each of the six sparking plugs. One, three, four and six were just warm. Two and five were cold as the tip of an Eskimo's tool. I needed to think no more. I knew. I opened the tool box, and spread out all the spanners on the grass.

'What are you going to do?' she said, as though she didn't already know.
'I am taking off the cylinder head,' I told her.
'Whatever for?'
'Because that engine's only running on four cylinders, not

six. Because I will find that those two dead cylinders have been blocked off and the pistons taken out.'

'What on earth do you mean?'

'I mean that someone has hidden something in those cylinders.'

'Ridiculous. If they did that, the engine wouldn't work.'

'Indeed it would. It would work very well, and it does work very well, but it's a bit down on power - as I would have discovered if I'd driven it myself.

'I agree, though, that it would take someone who knew about cars to think of such a hiding place. Someone like Black, for instance.

'He'd remember that back in nineteen forty seven, when Major Goldie Gardner, the record-breaker, wanted to attack 500 c.c. records, he used a six-cylinder MG engine with two cylinders blocked off to bring down the capacity to the size he needed. And it worked all right then. The car did just over a hundred and eighteen miles an hour and broke all the records it set out to break. This has worked all right, too. Up to now, that is.'

'I don't know what you are talking about,' said Victoria.

'Well, then you have nothing to fear.'

I took off the black plug leads and began to loosen the head nuts. She watched me for a moment. I hadn't loosened many when she said: 'I'll give you half.'

'I don't want half.'

'You mean you want it all?'

'I'll see what there is, first.'

'How much *do* you want?' she asked, her face suddenly pale in the sun. The skin had tightened on her skull. She looked as she'd look in twenty years, when youth had left her and all her lovers had gone; when there was nothing of the past but curl-edged photographs in an album and memories of a meeting by a Corsican lake and on a mountain road.

She should have stayed in her league, and not grown ambitious. She might have been happier as a housewife in Barnet or

Penge. I said nothing, but went on loosening the nuts. If she'd known more about cars she would have realised I was bluffing. I couldn't really drain all the water from the radiator on a Corsican hilltop. For where could I find any more to fill it up? Make my own?

'There was a jewel robbery in Hong Kong,' she began.

I stopped her.

'I know all that. And the diamonds are inside this engine. Tell me something I don't know.'

'I got frightened,' she said.

'What keeps many people good, is that they frighten more easily than others,' I reminded her.

I straightened up, ring spanner still in my hand, and poured myself more wine, and then threw the empty bottle over the bank.

Life, I thought, is one long confusion of ironies. A gang steal two million pounds of diamonds on the other side of the world. A pilot flies them out, and another man decides to bring down the plane. And then a third group of people, not even knowing there *are* any diamonds, decide to find out what was in that plane, on the basis that there must have been something of value or else why use a plane at all. And now here the loot was, two million quids' worth, only feet away.

'What are you going to do?' asked Victoria.

'You for a start,' I told her. 'But later. In my own time and my own way.'

'And then?'

'I suggest you disappear for your own good.'

'Why?'

'Because there'll be a reward offered. There always is. And I'm going to claim it. Possibly it will be about a hundred thousand quid, though I won't be greedy. I'll settle for less. Like ninety.'

'You bastard,' said Victoria flatly.

'I know. That's one of my family secrets. But then my family motto is: *Nihil illegitimae carborundum.* Don't let the bastards grind you down. Because they will, if you let them.

'But I'll give you what your husband promised you. Five thousand. That seems only fair. After all you've been through.'

She said nothing, but just stood there, looking at me. Now I poured her a glass of wine from the other bottle and we waited in the sun for Love to return. Love with a capital letter, of course. The other sort had never been there, and would never be there.

But I'd be there, and with all the strength of this reward, even if split down the middle between the doctor and me. And I still had the additional bonus of two old cars to be collected, when I could spare the time.

'You're smiling,' Victoria said.

'Yes,' I admitted. 'So would you be in my position.'

She emptied her glass.

'Just what *is* your position?' she asked softly.

So I put down my glass and showed her.

Swallowcliffe, Wiltshire; Venaco and Ajaccio, Corsica.

THE END

ABOUT THE AUTHOR

James Leasor

James Leasor was one of the bestselling British authors of the second half of the 20th Century. He wrote over 50 books including a rich variety of thrillers, historical novels and biographies.
His works included the critically acclaimed  The Red Fort, the story of the Indian Mutiny of 1957, The Marine from Mandalay, Boarding Party (made into the film The Sea Wolves starring Gregory Peck, David Niven and Roger Moore), The Plague and the Fire, and The One that Got Away (made into a film starring Hardy Kruger). He also wrote Passport to Oblivion (which sold over 4 million copies around the World and was filmed as Where the Spies Are, starring David Niven), the first of nine novels featuring Dr Jason Love, a Cord car owning Somerset GP called to aid Her Majesty's Secret Service in foreign countries, and another bestselling series about the Far Eastern merchant Robert Gunn in the 19th century. There were also sagas set in Africa and Asia, written under the pseudonym Andrew MacAllan, and tales narrated by an unnamed vintage car dealer in Belgravia, who drives a Jaguar SS100.

www.jamesleasor.com Follow on Twitter: @jamesleasor

BOOKS IN THIS SERIES

Aristo Autos

They Don't Make Them Like That Any More

They don't make them like that any more. Cars, that is. They don't, and they never will again. Which accounts for the enormous world-wide interest in old motors of every description, and the fantastic prices that they fetch. Behind this latest manifestation of the international antique trade, lies a strange and secret world, where dealers offer for sale cars they do not own, where rich collectors willingly pay thousands for some mechanical abortion that can barely drag itself up a hill without a following wind, simply because it's rare. Usually, hazards in this old-car business - as in any other - are run by the buyer. But there are also risks for those who sell – as the proprietor of Aristo Autos discovers. He deals exclusively in motoring exotica, and when he's unexpectedly offered one of the rarest cars of all, a supercharged Mercedes two-seater 540K, he buys it immediately. There's a clear two-and-a-half thousand quid profit for him in the deal. But soon he realises there's also a clear danger of death, for someone else desperately wants this car for some very special, private reason. Someone who will kill to get it. But who, and why? The only thing to do is to find out, and he does - travelling a sinister trail, blazed by old cars and young girls, that leads from London to Spain to Switzerland.

'Number one thriller on my list ...sexy and racy'

Sunday Mirror

'Devoured at a sitting... racy, pungent and swift'
The Sunday Times

'A racy tale... the hero spends most of his time trying to get into beds and out of trouble... plenty of action, anecdotes, and inside dope on exotic old cars'
Sunday Express

Never Had A Spanner On Her

In the sequel to "They Don't Make Them Like That Any More" our vintage car dealer gets involved in a scheme to import some vintage cars from Nasser's Egypt. From the run of the mill trades of London our hero finds himself in Cairo and trying to export a Bugatti Royale, probably the rarest car on the planet. The story has suspense, guns, a beautiful girl and of course masses of old cars. It races from Belgravia, to Belsize Park to the Pyramids and Alexandria. Leasor combines his proven thriller writing skills with an encyclopaedic knowledge of vintage cars to deliver a real page turner.

'Mr. Leasor has a delightful sense of the ridiculous; he also has an educated style which stems from more than 20 very good books.'
Manchester Evening News

'All good reading, with accurate detail of the cars involved.'
Autocar

'Vintage adventure for auto-lovers and others alike.' The Evening News

BOOKS BY THIS AUTHOR

Passport To Oblivion

Passport to Oblivion is the first case book of Dr. Jason Love . . . country doctor turned secret agent. Multi-million selling, published in 19 languages around the world and filmed as Where the Spies Are starring David Niven.

"Heir Apparent to the golden throne of Bond" The Sunday Times

Mandarin-Gold

It was the year of 1833 when Robert Gunn arrived on the China coast. Only the feeblest of defenses now protected the vast and proud Chinese Empire from the ravenous greed of Western traders, and their opening wedge for conquest was the sale of forbidden opium to the native masses.
This was the path that Robert Gunn chose to follow... a path that led him through a maze of violence and intrigue, lust and treachery, to a height of power beyond most men's dreams — and to the ultimate depths of personal corruption.
Here is a magnificent novel of an age of plunder — and of a fearless freebooter who raped an empire.

'Highly absorbing account of the corruption of an individual during a particularly sordid era of British imperial history,' The Sunday Times

Follow The Drum

'Once in a while, a book comes along that grabs you by the throat, shakes you, and won't let go until you have read through to the last page.' - Hal Burton, Newsday

'Follow the Drum is superb reading entertainment' - Best Sellers
India, in the mid-nineteenth century, was virtually run by a British commercial concern, the Honourable East India Company, whose directors would pay tribute to one Indian ruler and then depose another in their efforts to maintain their balance sheet of power and profit. But great changes were already casting shadows across the land, and when a stupid order was given to Indian troops to use cartridges greased with cow fat and pig lard (one animal sacred to the Hindus and the other abhorrent to Moslems) there was mutiny. The lives of millions were changed for ever including Arabella MacDonald, daughter of an English regular officer, and Richard Lang, an idealistic nineteen-year-old who began 1857 as a boy and ended it a man.

Open Secret

Max Cornell had survived the Katyn massacre and the Russian camps. Now he wanted a new life - and the money to enjoy it - in England. And the price of a passport was three years' work for British Intelligence, running the Russian codenamed Butcher.
Asimir Vasarov, once camp commandant at Katyn, became Stalin's closest aide - a man whose political loyalty was assured and whose power was unlimited.
But the successful British businessman and the man from the shadows of the Kremlin share more than memories of the past. In the post-war world of high politics and backstreet crime, they are linked by an explosive truth which could rock governments if it ever became an OPEN SECRET.

'Fast-moving... a nice seedy atmosphere' - SUNDAY EXPRESS

Tank Of Serpents

Benares, India, 1945. Captain Richard Blake stands trial at a court martial, accused of stealing a million rupees from one of the wealthiest, most powerful and dangerous men in India. Eight years later, he begins his quest for retribution...

'Unlike Jeffrey Archer, James Leasor seems to have a natural ease with words; and this fluency means that his book moves along at an altogether faster clip." The Times

'Well up to the standard we have come to expect from one of Britain's best thriller writers...a superb study of revenge!
Evening News

'A good, solid read!'
Daily Mail

Most books by James Leasor are now available as ebook and in paperbacks. Please visit www.jamesleasor.com for details on all these books or contact info@jamesleasor.com for more information on availability.

Follow on Twitter: @jamesleasor for details on new releases.

Jason Love novels
Passport to Oblivion (filmed, and republished in paperback, as Where the Spies Are)
Passport to Peril (Published in the U.S. as Spylight)
Passport in Suspense (Published in the U.S. as The Yang Meridian)
Passport for a Pilgrim
A Week of Love
Love-all
Love and the Land Beyond
Frozen Assets
Love Down Under

Jason Love and Aristo Autos novel
Host of Extras

Aristo Autos novels
They Don't Make Them Like That Any More
Never Had A Spanner On Her

Robert Gunn Trilogy
Mandarin-Gold
The Chinese Widow
Jade Gate

Other novels
Not Such a Bad Day

The Strong Delusion
NTR: Nothing to Report
Follow the Drum
Ship of Gold
Tank of Serpents

Non-fiction
The Monday Story
Author by Profession
Wheels to Fortune
The Serjeant-Major; a biography of R.S.M. Ronald Brittain, M.B.E., Coldstream Guards
The Red Fort
The One That Got Away
The Millionth Chance: The Story of The R.101
War at the Top (published in the U.S. as The Clock With Four Hands)
Conspiracy of Silence
The Plague and the Fire
Rudolf Hess: The Uninvited Envoy
Singapore: the Battle that Changed the World
Green Beach
Boarding Party (filmed, and republished in paperback, as The Sea Wolves)
The Unknown Warrior (republished in paperback as X-Troop)
The Marine from Mandalay
Rhodes & Barnato: the Premier and the Prancer

As Andrew MacAllan (novels)
Succession
Generation
Diamond Hard
Fanfare
Speculator
Traders

As Max Halstock
Rats – The Story of a Dog Soldier

Printed in Great Britain
by Amazon